D0039890

Spring of Tears

Cornelia Feye

FOR MAX AND SEBASTIAN

To Sharon,

kind regards,

Pamela Frye

April 2012

ACKNOWLEDGMENTS

Thanks to my husband Glen for his support, encouragement, and patience. My writing group members Edda Hodnett and Mary Kay Gardner have given me countless suggestions for improvements, and told me to cut out whatever was unnecessary. Thanks to Carol Buckley for cheerfully editing the original copy. Many thanks to Jean Lowe for going all the way to Mont Ste Odile in France, taking pictures of the Spring of Tears, and then allowing me to use her "Coors" amphora for the cover, which Maura Walters skillfully and creatively designed.

Prologue:

Sarah knew she was damaged. She had known since she was twelve years old, but she had never realized how deep the wound was. Somehow she had always thought maybe she'd get over it, or that she could escape and start over somewhere on another continent, in another city. But now it all came to an end, on a mountaintop, on a spring night. Finally it was all over. She did not have to run anymore, she did not have to hide and fight anymore. Briefly she thought about her brother, her father, and her niece. Then everything went black.

Tuesday, May 12, 9 AM, Mont Ste Odile Alsace, France:

Despite the fog it was going to be a wonderful day. Vega Stern was
determined to make it so as she trudged down the sodden forest
path, wet leaves squishing under her soles. She was living in France,
the country of her dreams and pursuing a story she had chosen to
write about the ancient abbess Ste Odile, who used to reside on this
mountain in the Alsace. On clear days Vega could see the Rhine
Valley, the Black Forest in Germany, and the spire of Strasbourg
Cathedral from here. Today she could barely see the next oak tree
along the slippery path before bumping into it. She took in a deep
breath of pungent-smelling forest air, moist and rich after the rain.
The brown discarded foliage from last fall formed a wet and soggy
carpet under her feet, cushioning every step she took. After
descending the slope for a few minutes Vega arrived at the Spring of
Tears, where healing waters sprang from the rocks leaving them
glistening and wet. For a while Vega watched the stream of water
burst from the rock and then disappear again between stones and
leaves. Its gurgling sound was muffled by the fog. Suddenly
something pink and pointy between the twigs and leaves caught her
eye. The light pink object stood out like a neon sign amidst the earthy
colors of green, brown, rust, and gray. Vega stepped closer. The
object was triangular and sharp-edged, and the closer she came, the
clearer she could see that it had very elegant lines.

Moving some leaves aside with the toe of her sneaker Vega saw a fancy and pointy ladies' sling back shoe. To be precise, it would have been a very fancy shoe without its broken heel and the ugly spots of discoloration on its side. It was a left shoe, without its companion.

"It's Gucci," Vega murmured quietly. She had a pair from the same label, and she loved them. Hers were black-and-white cowhide, with very pointy toes, and they had set her back quite a bit in her salary when she still held a regular job. Unfortunately she could not wear them for longer than an hour; they simply were too painful and turned her toes into a blistery mess. How could anybody walk the paths on Mont Ste Odile with shoes like that? No wonder the heel had broken and the wearer had taken them off. The spots were probably traces of mud from slipping on the moss. But why was there only one shoe? And why had the wearer left behind such an expensive model? And where, for heaven's sake, was the owner anyway?

Carefully, Vega picked up the shoe and looked at it more closely. Those spots were no regular mud discolorations. They were reddish brown; if Vega was not mistaken, they looked more like blood. It could have been blood from sore and bruised feet, but the spots were in an odd location, on the outside toward the back of the shoe, where abrasions usually don't occur. Vega decided to take a photograph of the shoe in its original location, before she gingerly put it into one of the canvas shopping bags, which she always carried in her purse, in case she had to stop for groceries. Her curiosity piqued she stalked around the spring for a little while, but could not find any interesting clues about the owner of the shoe or what had happened to her. Slightly rattled she sat down on one of the moss-covered stone benches in front of the spring. She took a deep breath of the moist and fresh air. A platform had been leveled and paved with flagstones for visitors to rest, pray, or

3

contemplate. Next to the murmuring spring a small shrine was carved into a rocky niche. It held a simple plaster figure of Ste Odile, now protected by several iron bars. Pilgrims and visitors had brought flowers and stuck them through the bars.

After thirteen centuries the influence of Ste Odile, the patroness of Alsace was still strong. She had been the daughter of Duke Aldrich, ruler of this whole region in the seventh century. When Odile was born blind her father rejected her. He rather wanted a son to succeed him on the throne. To protect the child from her father's anger the mother hid her in the convent of Palma, close to Besancon. At the age of twelve she was baptized by the bishop of Regensburg and given the name Odilia, daughter of light. After she returned to the Alsace, Odile prayed at the spring for the soul of her pagan father. As she cried for him, she soothed her eyes with the water from the spring and suddenly gained her eyesight. A miracle had happened that thirteen hundred years later still drew many pilgrims, particularly those with eye problems, to the site. Eventually Odile softened her father's heart, and he finally gave her his fortress Hohenburg, which she transformed into a convent. [1]

Vega was working on an article for the *Alsatian Monthly* about the miraculous lady of the mountain. Odile had used her newly acquired sight to study manuscripts and sacred texts and became a very well educated nun, who turned her convent into a small university, a place of learning for women. She

---

[1] According to another version of the legend, Odilia gained her eyesight during her baptism at age 13.

had been graced with the physical benefit of sight but also used her gift to enlighten the minds of those who sought her presence during the Dark Ages. Her article was due in seven days and she was still floundering. At deadline she had to submit fifteen hundred words about the history of the convent and its former abbess, complete with photographs of the scenic view atop the mountain to make it appealing to visitors, tourists, and locals alike. She had come here for inspiration, but unfortunately she could not concentrate. Her mind kept asking the same question over and over again: how had an elegant and stylish pink shoe found its way to this ancient and sacred site?

Vega climbed the forest path back up from the spring to the convent, which stood like the fortress it had once been on the top of the mountain. Now nuns no longer lived inside the convent walls. The former cells were part of a hostel, catering mainly to pilgrims and visitors who valued a quiet retreat in a deeply spiritual place over luxury and noisy entertainment. Vega herself had spent a weekend at the Ste Odile Hotel and remembered the vast and quiet view from her window at sunset and the sparkling night sky, far away from any electrical light.

The steps on the path were slippery with wet moss, and Vega was glad she wore sneakers with rubber soles. She reached the former fortress's giant arched wooden gates, locked each night between ten o'clock and reopened at ten in the morning, and walked across the tree-studded courtyard toward the northeast corner of the monastery. For her article she had promised to include images and stories of the Chapel of Angels and the Chapel of Tears, which were perched precariously on the edge of the mountain. The chapels were two small stone structures, no larger than ten square meters. The interiors of both were covered with gold mosaic in the Byzantine style, depicting the spheres of cherubs and seraphim circling the throne of God, as well as beautifully patterned plants and details of a strange and otherworldly landscape. Vega entered the Chapel of Angels and studied the gold mosaic patterns, which covered the small and dimly lit interior for a while, but her mind strayed. The pink shoe seemed to burn in her purse. Images of a young, stylish woman in a pink suit stumbling down the slippery steps toward the spring popped into her mind.

She sighed and exited the chapels to the viewing terrace. Light gray cumulus clouds partially covered the sky, moving rapidly across it and letting rays of sun escape only intermittently. Vega sat down on a bench, now deserted since there was nothing really to see, except for fog and clouds, and opened her notebook. She hadn't gotten very far yet with her article. All she had written fit on one page.

Odile closed her eyes to feel the moist fog on her face. She remembered the first twelve years of her life, when she had experienced the world around her only through the sense of touch, smell, and sound. While she was blind, her nose, ears, and hands had been her only pathways to the world around her. Sometimes she retreated back to those days and tried to recreate the heightened sense of awareness that had been her own. Her mind had been an expansive space, filled only with the images of her soul. Those images were lucid and crystalline in nature, like stained glass windows, shimmering in brilliant reds, golds, and aquamarine. People pitied her for her affliction, but she was in a constant state of awe. In her mind's eye, she had seen the spheres of the cherubs and seraphim circling around the throne of God. Here on this spot in the Hohenburg she wanted to recreate those images in a small chapel devoted to the sacred geometry of the heavens. She envisioned golden mosaic placed in a semi-dark chapel so that the eyes had to adjust and activate their concentration on the invisible world. Odile opened her eyes and let her gaze penetrate the mist. The forest of the Vogesen spread in

front of her, and she could see the small villages of Barr and Obernai beneath her. The rolling landscape of the Alsace opened itself up to her like a precious scroll in the convent library. She followed it all the way to the Rhine Valley. This landscape told her story and it told the story of those before her and it would tell the story of those who would live here long after she was gone.

With a frown Vega closed the notebook. After rereading the paragraph she realized that it definitely would not do. She had to come up with something a lot more substantial and contemporary for her contribution to the *Alsatian Monthly*. Checking her watch she realized that she had plenty of time before she had to pick up her two sons from the International School in Strasbourg. Four precious hours stretched in front of her. Time in which she could write, shop, drive around the beautiful Alsace landscape, take walks through small villages along the Route du Vin, and do research for her article. But she really did not want to do any of those things right now. She just wanted to know how the pink shoe ended up next to the Spring of Tears.

Feeling the fresh, cool air on her face, she briskly retraced her steps to the almost deserted parking lot just below the abbey. Her small blue Volkswagen Polo stood alone amidst the empty field. Vega folded her tall body into the small car and slipped out of her sneakers with the rubber soles and into a pair of two-tone pointy sling backs. She followed the scenic route D854, which wound its way down the mountain on narrow switchbacks. Dark pine trees obscured the view while she descended, and white fog with the consistency of cotton candy hung heavily between the trees. Vega gave up hope that she would be rewarded with a spectacular panorama today.

Driving into the small village of Obernai at the foot of Mont Ste Odile, Vega decided to stop in at the *Golden Swan*, an old-fashioned *Gaststube*, for a café au lait. As Vega entered the restaurant, the owner, Madame Merrier, who had just opened, was still busy polishing glasses, stacking plates, and piling up freshly washed and starched white linen napkins behind her counter for the soon-to-be-expected lunch guests. The aroma of freshly brewed coffee filled the room and the clinking of the silverware and china made Vega feel comforted and relaxed

"Bonjour, Madame Stern," Mme. Merrier exclaimed cheerfully. Vega's answer was somewhat subdued, and she ordered a coffee, and after a short hesitation, a cognac as well. Mme. Merrier looked up startled and cast a quick glance at the wooden grandfather clock in the corner before reaching for the cognac tumbler.

"Yes, I know it is only eleven o'clock, but I've had a bit of a shock this morning," Vega confessed.

"*Mais, bien sur,*" Mme. Merrier bristled, obviously relieved that there was a simple explanation for this early alcohol consumption.

"I hope it is nothing serious?" she asked as she placed a big white coffee cup with its steaming froth of milk in front of Vega, next to a generously poured cognac.

"I hope not either," Vega confided, and seeing the worried look on the formidable Mme. Merrier's face, she thought it better to fess up. Mme. Merrier was not one to trifle with. She had an enormous bosom, which she tended to accentuate by wearing tight belts and figure-hugging sweaters. Her brown eyes looked kindly but intently at her customers, and missed nothing about their mood or their alcohol blood level, which was the reason why her customers usually made it home safely from even the most sumptuous lunches or dinners at the Golden Swan. Vega showed her the shoe and told her where she had found it. Mme. Merrier nodded her heavily coiffed hair gravely. Not a strand of her stiffly hair-sprayed hairdo moved.

"I think this is a case for Monsieur Bonacourt," she finally pronounced.

Vega observed with interest that she had poured herself a glass of cognac as well.

"Maybe it is just a fluke: a young girl and her boyfriend drive up to Mont Ste Odile after a party; they are a little tipsy; she takes off her high heels and decides to walk back barefoot!" Vega considered.

"Quite possible," admitted Mme. Merrier, "but unlikely."

"Why is it unlikely?" Vega asked, surprised.

"First of all, if she had walked to the spring in these shoes, the heel would have broken off a lot earlier, and secondly, these spots do not look like mud to me." Vega sighed slightly.

"I admit I had a similar suspicion. They looked like dried blood to me. But again, there can be a harmless explanation for that as well."

"Of course, but if there is a harmless explanation, then Monsieur Bonacourt will find it."

"Who is Monsieur Bonacourt? You seem to have a lot of confidence in him."

"Monsieur Bonacourt is one of my oldest and best customers," Mme. Merrier pronounced proudly, as if that was qualification enough. "In addition, he is also the *commissario generell* in Hagenau," she concluded triumphantly.

"He wouldn't want to bother with a single pink shoe—" Vega protested, but Mme. Merrier cut her off.

"Monsieur Bonacourt comes here every Wednesday and Friday for lunch. Wednesdays, I bake my onion tart, and Fridays, we get fresh venison and game. You could come here around one o'clock, and I'll introduce you, so you can bring up the topic casually."

"I might do that, Madame Merrier. Thank you."

Mme. Merrier nodded, confident that she had resolved all the problems and questions that could arise before noon, and was now giving her full attention to the real task at hand: getting ready for lunch.

Vega paid and left. As she cruised between the gentle hills of Haut-Rhin toward Strasbourg, she contemplated what to do next. It was too late to go home, too early to pick up the kids. She cursed herself for her indecision. It was not like her. She used to be a professional woman with a career and appointments all day. She had given it all up to live in her beautiful dream house in the French countryside, and now she found herself floundering. It was not easy to live her dream. She could not quite resign herself to a role as housewife and mother, but she obviously did not have quite what it took to be a writer either.

As was to be expected, she was soon stuck in the lunchtime traffic heading east toward the Rhine and the German border. Vega closed her eyes briefly and took a deep breath trying to release the stress of sitting in a traffic jam. Being blocked by cars on all sides, unable to move, triggered her claustrophobia. She remembered reading somewhere that breathing exercises helped to steady nerves. Therefore she slowly counted to four while breathing in, and then after a pause, released her breath to an equal count. This exercise however did not work at all, and she resorted to the time-proven method of biting her nails instead, which always seemed to make her feel better. The French drivers around her reacted with an equal lack of contemplation and patience, and their car horns blared angrily. Vega reigned in her thoughts and tried to direct them onto the road in front of her, but they kept straying to the pink shoe in her bag, so she decided she might as well go to Strasbourg to her favorite shoe store.

Tuesday, May 12, 11:30 AM, Strasbourg, France:

Stefani's Marché du Chaussure was located at the Place de l'Homme de Fer, the central shopping area of Strasbourg, in the old town center close to the cathedral. It was impossible to drive or park anywhere even close to the store, so Vega left her car near the Place de Bordeaux, not far from her children's Ecole International and took the tram. For a medieval city like Strasbourg the trams were surprisingly futuristic, with streamlined cars, mostly consisting of warped panoramic windows and comfortably upholstered seats. In addition they were quiet and on time! Alsace, the small piece of land between France and Germany, had many advantages. Not only was it geographically located in the temperate and beautiful Rhine Valley, which made it ideal for growing fruity wines, but it also combined German efficiency with French cooking and lifestyle. Vega sank onto a comfortably upholstered tram bench. What was she trying to accomplish? She would just go into the store, and see if they carried this particular model of shoe, or if she could find any clue about its owner. Little chance of that. If they had ever even carried the shoe, the sales clerks would surely not remember any customer who had bought it! Maybe she just needed an excuse for going to a shoe store. The tram came to a silent and smooth halt and Vega got out.

At this hour, Stefani's was still relatively empty, and as Vega entered the store, a gorgeous young sales clerk approached her. She had short henna-red hair, was taller than Vega, and dressed in a black miniskirt, which revealed endlessly long, slim legs, and lime green open-toe mules. A discreet nametag pinned to her tight black sweater, barely long enough to conceal her belly button, informed Vega that the young woman's name was Nicole. The young woman stared hard at Vega, who became uncomfortable under such scrutiny. She was grateful that she had taken off her sneakers before coming here; she tried to stare back, but could not help feeling slightly provincial and disheveled next to this elegant creature.

Obviously satisfied with her effect, Nicole asked with the slightest of smiles, "Can I help you, madame?"

"Well, yes, maybe." Vega pulled out her canvas shopping bag. "This shoe, does it look familiar?" Vega showed the pink slipper to Nicole holding on to the shoe with a part of the canvas bag, as not to add unnecessary fingerprints to the surface. She thought that this girl had probably started working here two days ago and would not recognize anything.

"You lost the other one?" Nicole asked unperturbed.

"It's kind of a long story. Do you, or did you, carry this model?" Vega inquired.

"Tsk-tsk," Nicole clucked, "it is in bad shape, is it not?"

She is like my children, Vega thought: answering a question with another question.

"Maybe I should just look around," Vega suggested.

"No, no, madame, you will not find this shoe anymore," Nicole pronounced with sudden authority, and walked briskly over to the shoe shelves. She pulled out a pair of sling-back shoes in a similar but slightly more artificial looking shade of pink and held it next to Vega's dilapidated piece of evidence.

"You see, you have last season's model. The color is different and so is the heel. It is a little higher, and is angled more sharply toward the front of the shoe."

"Yes, now that you point it out, I can see it. How long ago did you sell this kind of shoe?" Vega inquired innocently.

"We sold the last pair only a couple of weeks ago. It was on sale, as it dates from last season." At least Nicole knew what she was talking about.

"May I inquire how much it cost?" Vega ventured. Nicole looked at her contemptuously. She despised women who talked about prices, and this one wanted to know about the prices of last season's sale merchandise on top of it!

"May I inquire why you want to know that," Nicole countered, "seeing that the shoe is not available anymore?"

"Mainly curiosity. Do you have any other shoes from last season on sale?"

Without a word, Nicole stalked over to the sales rack, swinging her hips like a fashion model on the runway in the process, and pointed at the reduced merchandise. Then she raised her eyebrows and disappeared behind a door with the word *Private* marked on it without even the shortest glance back. Vega fingered a pair of turquoise Gucci sling-backs, which even in their reduced state cost 275 Euros.

Tuesday, May 12, 3:30 PM, Klingenthal:

By the time Vega drove into the small village of Klingenthal with her two boys in the backseat of the car, clouds completely covered the sky and a drizzling rain made it hard to maneuver the slick country roads.

"How was school?" she asked over her shoulder. Daniel, her twelve-year-old merely grunted.

"Excellent, Mom," answered Steven, Vega's seven-year old son, perkily.

"I founded my own company."

"Oh yeah? What is it called?"

"It's called TMC Inc."

"Does that stand for something specific?"

"Of course, Mom. It stands for 'Toys, Money, and Cards.'"

"I should have known. What does the company do?"

"Mom, isn't that obvious? We make toys, money, and cards."

"Yes, of course. How is business?"

"Pretty good. I am the manager of the card division, Harry is the boss, and then we have workers, of course."

"Yes, you need those, I am sure," Vega commented, not wanting to curb his entrepreneurial zeal.

"Who are the workers and what do they do?"

"They make the toys, mostly, but we had to fire one today."

"Really, who was he and why was he fired?"

"It was Charlie. Harry fired him because he didn't make enough money."

"That's a popular reason for firing people, I suppose."

"Mom, how do you make money?"

"Well, you earn it, by doing chores for example."

"No, I mean, how do you *make* money?"

"I see what you mean. You want to go into the forgery business. Actually, only the government can make—that means print—money."

"I already made a million Euros. Want to see it?"

"I am driving, but sure, I'd like to see it."

"Here it is. Can I have some change?"

"You probably want Euro nine hundred ninety-nine thousand, nine hundred ninety-nine, right?

"How did you know?" Stevie asked delightedly and giggled. "Okay, I guess you don't have change. I'll work on my product catalogue then."

"How about homework? Did your teacher just watch your business transactions all day without teaching you anything important?"

"This is important. Daddy always says you have to start your own company. Plus we had a substitute teacher."

"That explains it."

"What did you do all day?"

"I went to Mont Ste Odile."

"Again?" both boys shouted incredulously in unison.

"Yes, I am still working on my article."

"How boring!" they yawned.

Vega had just considered telling them that she had by no means had a boring morning, when their driveway came into view, and the little white mutt, Mona, welcomed them with excited barks. Vega let the boys out so they could run the last meters of the way with the dog that was overjoyed to see her young masters.

As Vega drove up to the house, she felt a moment of joy and a slight acceleration of her heartbeat. This house was her dream come true: a hundred-year-old stone farmhouse, situated on top of a shallow hill, with vineyards descending from its southern side, where a porch extended along the entire length of the building. Its support beams were overgrown with grapevines. Vega and her husband had taken out the dividing walls on the ground floor of the building, which now consisted of one large, bright room with hardwood floors and very little furniture. There was a grand fireplace, Moroccan rugs on the floor, and a nineteen century ottoman, which was everybody's favorite place, including Mona's. Besides large Moroccan pillows on the ground, there was a big wooden table with ten straight-back chairs between the living room and the open kitchen, where most of the Stern family activities took place. The few furnishings were perfectly sufficient, and their simplicity was balanced by the abundance of art on the walls. Mostly they were paintings, drawings, and prints done by artist friends of the family, including some masterpieces of the children, but a Joan Miró and a Paul Klee painting had found their way there as well. After feeding the children some snacks and settling them down for their homework, Vega walked upstairs to the second floor to her bedroom to put away her purse and backpack. Her glance fell out of the window toward the north face of the house, where their small orchard of almond and cherry trees was in full bloom. The pink flowers on the branches seemed to float in the gray sky like lotus blossoms on a river, their color intensified by the lack of direct sunlight, their rosy color advancing toward her in front of the gray background. It made them look sad and exaggeratedly cheerful at the same time. Vega pulled the shoe from her backpack. It had the same color as the blossoms.

Wednesday, May 13, Klingenthal, 10 AM

After dropping off the children at school the next morning, Vega had no spell of indecision at all. The sky was as bright and clear as her mind, and spring birds sat on blooming trees and chattered excitedly. She drove purposefully up the mountain to the monastery of Ste Odile. The gate was wide open, and she got several excellent photos of the view from the terrace, and several mediocre pictures of the interior of the Chapels of Tears and Angels. At last she had come up with a new angle to write about the mosaics; she would use the depiction of herbs and plants in the mosaics to make them more interesting and relevant to twenty-first century readers. Since many of those readers would be Alsatian, who therefore placed a high priority on anything to do with food, she could focus on the wild strawberries and bitter herbs depicted in the Chapel of Tears. As much as their symbolic value in religious art spoke of Christ's suffering and redemption, they were also ingredients in fruit tarts and asparagus sauces!

Feeling very productive and efficient, Vega was ready to leave around eleven o'clock. She considered going back down to the Spring of Tears but could not quite bring herself to do so. It was too early to leave for lunch, and the tourists were beginning to crowd into the convent courtyard, filling it with exclamations in French, German, and English, so Vega hesitantly moved toward the gate and turned left in the direction of the prehistoric Pagan Wall. Few tourists found their way to this path, which led through the forest alongside the ten-kilometer-long ancient wall constructed of interlocking stones with tenons as the connecting pieces. For a casual visitor neither its age nor its intricate construction method was apparent, as the wall was overgrown by moss and vines and reached its full height of four meters only in rare places. But Vega appreciated its quiet mystery, and often wondered what it had once protected. What had been so important thousands of years before the birth of Christ that an elaborately long and time-consuming wall had to be constructed around it? No fortress lay within its confines, no ancient city, just a few graves and a small pond, sacred to the eye and water goddess, where Druids might have touched pilgrims' eyes with water for healing and enlightenment. Or they might have sacrificed lambs and possibly other victims to the ancient goddess, believing that their tears brought fertility. On a day like this, nothing hinted at sinister rituals along the pagan wall. The air smelled of fresh growth and the leave-covered ground was dappled in sunlight filtering through the bright green leaves of the oak and beech trees. Vega wanted to weave a clever connection into her article about Odile's Spring of Tears and the pagan eye and water goddess, who had been worshipped on this mountain thousands of years before Odile's time.

The cry of a cuckoo interrupted Vega's thoughts and, as she felt the warmth of the intermittent sunbeams on her back, she was conscious that spring was really here. Fresh new spring leaves glistened clean and shiny in the morning sun. Vega wished she had worn practical footwear, instead of having to deal with drops of moisture seeping into her purple mules. Feeling the wetness penetrate her soles, she was reminded of the pink slipper and a trace of anxiety entered her mind. She tried to picture the owner of the shoe. It had to have been a young woman, wearing size 7 1/2 shoes, the same as her own. Why had the young woman come to this forest in those shoes? What had been the purpose of her descent to the Spring of Tears? Vega scanned the path in front of her, trying to avoid unnecessary puddles or muddy spots, when her eye suddenly fell on an alien object in this ancient landscape. There was a faint glitter and an edge of ugly white plastic, contrasting sharply with the fresh wetness of the ground. Vega bent down to get a closer look; half of the object was hidden underneath a brown oak leaf. She pushed it aside with a twig and revealed a used syringe. It was empty except for a small amount of blood left in the compressed chamber of the syringe. Next to the implement lay a latex string that must have been used as a tourniquet to tie the arm and enlarge the target veins.

"Junkies," muttered Vega. She felt slightly revolted but nevertheless picked up the syringe with the help of a tissue and placed it into a plastic shopping bag she found in her purse. She did not want any hiker, or child touching the needle by accident. Who knew what contamination it contained?

Vega straightened up and tried to assess her exact location. She had walked about twenty minutes from the entrance gate of the convent. On her way she had passed a turnoff leading directly to the spring of Ste Odile, a little way down the mountain. She turned to go back. Suddenly the fresh lime green leaves did not look so appealing anymore. Suddenly the clean-swept sky did not seem so innocent and promising anymore. Suddenly the Pagan Wall's secret did not feel so ancient anymore. Events had taken place in very recent times, maybe just a few days ago, involving unhappy and possibly endangered people. Vega hated to think of her adopted home, the country of her dreams, as another place where drugs had taken root and were ruining lives. "Maybe there is a harmless explanation," she thought, which reminded her of M. Bonacourt and Mme. Merrier's special onion tart, which would be just about ready to come out of the oven at this moment. Slightly cheered by the thought, Vega hurried back to her car and drove down the hill to the *Golden Swan.*

Wednesday, May 13, 1 PM, Obernai:

As Vega opened the door to enter the *Gaststube,* noisily chattering voices and the smell of fresh baking greeted her. At the counter stood a portly man, in a slightly shabby but still elegant olive green suit. As he turned toward her she could see that his trousers were a little too tight around his waist. His gray, curly, and unruly hair framed a pink face and gave him the dynamic appearance of a concert conductor. He wore thick-framed glasses, and a bushy gray mustache topped his full lips. He licked the latter, as he set down with flourish a glass stein, from which he had no doubt just taken a large sip of Alsatian beer.

"Bonjour, Madame Stern," Mme. Merrier called out to her from behind the counter. "May I introduce you to Monsieur Bonacourt, *commissario generell* of Hagenau!" she added proudly.

"A pleasure to meet you, monsieur. Madame Merrier speaks very highly of you," Vega said as she approached and shook the inspector's outstretched hand.

"*Merci beaucoup!* Mme. Merrier tells me you are a writer?"

"Well, I am sort of a free-lance writer and I am working on an article about Mont Ste Odile…"

"Ah, yes, the magic mountain of the Alsace! So many stories happened on that mountain, in ancient times and some only a few hundred years ago…" he pondered with great enthusiasm. "What publication are you writing for?"

"It is for the *Alsatian Monthly*'s German language edition. It is about the lasting influence of Saint Odile and the cultural importance of the abbey." That did not sound so bad, Vega thought, now she just had to actually pull it off.

"I am a bit of a hobby historian myself. Nothing too serious, but I am greatly interested in the history of our Mont Ste Odile."

"I am an art historian. That's why the Chapel of Angels and Chapel of Tears are of particular interest to me," Vega admitted.

"Would you join me for lunch? We can talk about your research. I am sure you have some fascinating stories to tell…"

Vega cringed inwardly, thinking how little she actually had written for her article.

"Actually I'd like to ask you a question about a story that might have happened very recently on Mont Ste Odile."

"Of course, of course. We will have Madame Merrier's delicious onion tart and talk about one of my favorite subjects, the art and culture of the Alsace, and of course its excellent cuisine."

There was no need to order their food, since Mme. Merrier already knew what they wanted and would have been greatly insulted had they even considered eating anything else than her famous onion tart.

"I want to show you something . . ." Vega began, but at that moment, Mme. Merrier arrived with the steaming, crisp onion tarts, served with spinach salad and apple cider, and after appropriate exclamations of delight, they had to devote several silent minutes to the house specialty, which melted in their mouths crisp and tart and hinting of ham and cheese, and other utterly secret ingredients.

"What do you want to show me, Madame?" asked M. Bonacourt wiping his huge mustache with a napkin.

"It is a shoe, monsieur. I hesitate to put it onto the table next to the food." She pushed the empty plates aside with her arm.

"I am not an expert on shoes, as you can imagine—" M. Bonacourt began, but Vega interrupted him and laid the Ziploc bag containing the pink slipper in front of him onto the table.

"I found this shoe at the spring of Ste Odile yesterday. As you see it is broken and has strange discolorations on the side. It is only half of the pair, and I found it strange and suspicious enough to show it to you."

"Ah, you found it at the Spring of Tears, you say?" M. Bonacourt's face and voice were suddenly serious.

"Yes, that's one of the aspects I found disturbing. Who would climb down the slippery path to the spring in shoes like this?"

"Indeed, this would be an uncomfortable and most likely unsuccessful descent. But this might in fact be the explanation to the abandoned shoe. Assume its owner realized that she could not master the slippery trail in her footwear, therefore she kicked them off and continued bare-footed."

"Yes, I considered that as well, but this is an Italian designer shoe and it costs even on sale two hundred seventy-five Euros. Why would she throw away such an expensive object?"

"Madame, you see it is broken and stained. Maybe that is the reason it was discarded."

"What about the stain? It looks like blood to me!" Vega objected.

"The laboratory would have to test it and detect its consistency. But it could just as well be muddy water from the recent rains."

"Why would anybody in their right mind hike down Mont Ste Odile in these shoes?" Vega felt exasperated now.

"Madame, unfortunately, not everybody is of sound mind these days," M. Bonacourt pronounced philosophically.

"Ah, and then today I found this!" she said triumphantly and pulled out the small bag with the syringe. M. Bonacourt smiled.

"Another piece of evidence, yes?" he asked indulgently.

"I found it next to the Pagan Wall, half hidden by leaves."

"Unfortunate, but not entirely unusual," said the inspector with a trace of regret in his voice. "Even in our quaint Alsace we do encounter drugs here and there."

"Well," concluded Vega, who had suddenly run out of things to say, "I suppose I have taken up enough of your time. I also need to pick up my children from school."

"Madame, if it makes you feel better, I will send a couple of officers to Mont Ste Odile tomorrow to look around the Spring." he said graciously but added in a patronizing tone, "It would have been preferable to leave the evidence where you originally found it."

Feeling foolish and angry, Vega got up, taking the bag and the shoe with her.

Wednesday, May 13, en route to Klingenthal, 3:15 PM:

By the time she had the kids safely in the backseat of her car, Vega had calmed down and put the matter of the shoe out of her mind. During the drive home Stevie explained survival strategies to Daniel and her.

"Do you know what is most important if you want to survive in quicksand?" he asked rhetorically, knowing full well that no member in his family possessed this kind of expertise.

Playing along, Vega asked gamely, "What is most important?"

"You have to carry a large wooden stick with you at all times!" Stevie exclaimed with great emphasis.

"And why is that, Stevie?"

"Because if you fall into quicksand, you can hold on to the stick, and then you can work your leg over the stick or you press the stick down under you, so you can sit on it and you won't sink. Also, you can point the stick to your rescuers so they can grab it and pull you out!"

"That is very useful, Stevie, I'll remember that next time I enter quicksand."

"That's so stupid!" Daniel interjected. "There is no quicksand here or anywhere else we've ever been!"

"It's better to know what to do before it happens, because you don't want to be caught by surprise!" countered Steven undeterred. "I can also tell you how to eat disgusting, live creatures without throwing up!"

"Why would I want to eat disgusting live creatures, for crying out loud?" Daniel shouted, really angry now.

"Yes, Stevie, why would we want to do that?"

"Well, first of all, you may be on a television show and they give you earthworms to eat, or even cockroaches, and you have to do it or else you lose the game and a million dollars."

"I don't think we are going to be on that kind of a television show anytime soon." Vega tried to keep her voice very calm and soothing.

"The other reason is that you might be out in nature, lost and without any food, and all you have are worms or cockroaches, and you have to eat them to survive!"

"I don't want to listen to this anymore. It is really disgusting!" Daniel interrupted, tired of the conversation.

"Exactly, it's so disgusting that you should just swallow them whole; don't use your tongue at all. That's the only way to do it!"

"Thanks, Stevie; I'll keep that in mind the next time I have to eat earthworms!" Vega's irony was of course completely lost on Stevie, who nodded satisfied in the backseat, while Daniel made angry but indistinct noises next to him.

Thursday, May 14, 10 AM, Klingenthal:

On Thursday morning Vega worked on her article right after dropping off the kids. She sat at her computer, slightly distracted, and glanced out to the blooming cherry trees in front of her window, when the phone rang. Expecting a call from her husband, who was on a business trip in Ireland, she grabbed the receiver.

"Madame Stern?" Not her husband's voice, but familiar.

"Oui?"

"This is Inspector Bonacourt, madame. Excuse me for disturbing you at home."

"Yes?" Vega said curtly.

"We followed up on your suggestion and two police officers searched the area around the Spring of Tears this morning. I think we found the owner of the pink slipper."

"Oh, I am very relieved."

"She is dead!" There was a long pause.

"What happened to her?" Vega finally asked.

"We are not quite sure yet. The autopsy will tell us more, but I would like to ask you a few more questions and collect the shoe, which has now become evidence in the investigation."

"Who was she?"

"We don't know, madame; so far Cinderella has no name. Is it convenient for me to come by with an officer and talk about the details of your find?"

"Yes, of course. When? Do you know where I live?"

"Yes, madame, we are actually already on our way."

Unable to stay at her desk after this phone call, Vega paced nervously up and down her living room. True to his word, the inspector knocked at her door only 15 minutes after his call. Vega asked him and a uniformed officer, whom he introduced as Sergeant Mallarmé, into the living room.

"Coffee?" she asked.

"No, merci, I think we will just get right down to business," explained M. Bonacourt.

"Of course. Here is the shoe." She pushed the Ziploc bag across the table toward Bonacourt. "How did she die?"

"I would also like the other piece of evidence you showed me yesterday, madame. The victim was found with needle marks in her arm, most obviously caused by a syringe."

Vega looked him straight in the eye

"I threw it out, after showing it to you. You seemed to dismiss it as unimportant and I did not want the kids to get a hold of it."

"I apologize, madame, I did not understand the importance of what you showed me until today!" Vega got up silently and walked over to her garbage can. The uniformed officer followed and they managed to extract the syringe from carrot peels and coffee grains.

"When exactly did you find the shoe?" the inspector asked.

"It was on Tuesday morning, around nine-thirty. The gates of the monastery were still closed."

"Thank you, this is important. We may have to interview the guests there, but the time of death seems to have occurred between two and four o'clock in the morning on Tuesday. If the autopsy confirms this time, the overnight guests at Sainte Odile are in the clear, because the convent was closed between ten o'clock on Monday night and ten on Tuesday morning. Where exactly did you find the shoe?"

"To the left of the spring, a little ways back toward the incline. It was partially covered by wet leaves. I actually took a picture of the exact location before I picked it up."

"That was very wise of you, and it seems to be consistent with the location where we found the body. It had been dragged into the forest, and hidden behind the stone shrine and some shrubs. Badly hidden I may add."

"Someone killed her?"

"So it seems. Her killer dragged her into the forest. At the time she must have been either dead or unconscious; there is no sign of struggle, but there are marks on her legs and arms where she scraped along the ground. She must have lost her shoe in the process."

"Maybe she was still alive?" Vega asked, horrified.

"Madame, don't let your imagination go wild about this. There are still a lot of unknown factors. I think this is all we need from you today. We will test the blood in the syringe and compare it to the victim's."

"Who was she?"

"We don't know yet, madame. There was no identification, no purse, no money or driver's license."

"Someone robbed her!" Vega concluded.

"Apparently, Madame Stern. Her fingerprints and blood sample may tell us more."

"How did she look?" Vega asked suddenly.

"She was in her mid-thirties, blond, stylish, thin, too thin. Obviously we don't know the eye color."

"Why not?" Vega asked.

"Her eyes were cut out!" Bonacourt remarked.

"Could I see a picture of her?" Vega asked. Bonacourt looked at her sharply for a moment but then relented. He nodded to the officer next to him. Sergeant Mallarmé pulled a photograph out of his briefcase and laid it on the table. Vega realized that she had never seen a corpse, except on television, but this was different. The face in front of her was drained of color and blood, giving it a gray, almost metallic appearance, with lips of a blue-purple tint. The skin seemed to be pulled too tightly over the sharp, high cheekbones. A black blind had been laid over the part of the face where the eyes had been. Short, blond hair with highlights fell into the high forehead. The features were expressionless; No sign of struggle or pain was apparent, and the face looked eerily at peace and beautiful in a frozen sort of way.

After Vega had stared at the face silently for a minute, the inspector asked gently,

"Have you ever seen this face before?"

" I am sure I never met the woman in person, but I think I have seen this face before. I just don't remember where. Maybe in a magazine?"

"If you remember please let us know!" the inspector prompted.

"I will." Vega promised.

"Your photo of the shoe's original location will also be greatly appreciated," the inspector said as he handed her his card.

Vega nodded. "I will print it out for you. Will you please keep me informed, inspector?"

Bonacourt nodded formally and got up, concluding the interview.

Vega walked them to the door and watched the blue Renault with the two police officers drive away. But the image of the dead girl without eyes being dragged through the wet forest would not go away so easily. Where had she seen that face before? Was her dream turning into a nightmare?

Friday, May 15, Obernai, 10 AM:

When Vega dropped by the *Golden Swan* for a cup of *café au lait* Mme. Merrier waved her over to the counter conspiratorially.

"So, they identified the body!" she whispered triumphantly. When Vega raised her eyebrows doubtfully, Mme. Merrier nodded to herself, smiling self-importantly.

"Oh, I hear things. The inspector was here when a call came through on his cell phone, and he had to rush off, saying '*Très bien*, identification so soon!'"

"I am glad, I could be of use," said Vega calmly.

Now Mme. Merrier's eyebrows shot up.

"You had something to do with it? I should have known," she added somewhat indignantly, because a small detail of this investigation had eluded her.

"Oh, it was just a small hint that I was able to supply and which pointed the investigation in the right direction," said Vega vaguely and with false modesty, steaming inwardly that the innkeeper knew more than her!

"I suppose that is all you can say right now?" Mme. Merrier said, and after a short regretful nod by Vega, continued, "I am sure you will tell me · more, when you find out." She smiled confidentially.

"Yes, of course, Madame Merrier," Vega said obediently. "I have to go."

"I know you do, Madame Stern," concluded Mme. Merrier confidently and cleared away Vega's big, white coffee cup, which had earlier appeared unprompted.

Through the gushing rain Vega ducked into her car and immediately opened her cell phone, while looking through her wallet for the inspector's card. "I should not feel slighted," she thought, "this is not about me. This is a murder investigation, and my pride and curiosity have no place in it." Nevertheless, she dialed the inspector's cell number tensely and waited for an answer, while looking through her fogged windshield at the pouring rain pounding on the glass.

"Oui?" Inspector Bonacourt's voice answered curtly.

"It's Vega Stern, inspector."

"Madame Stern, we were able to identify the victim. She was a model as you suspected. We showed the picture to a few modeling agencies and they ran it through their databases."

"Who was she?"

"She was registered in a boarding house in the Rue de L'Outre, here in Strasbourg. She had been missing for three days."

"That sounds like a match."

"Yes, her landlady already identified the photo; we are just waiting for identification by her brother, who lives in Germany."

"She was German?"

"Yes," the inspector said haltingly. "I am sorry, but I have to go; I am at the morgue right now, but I'll call you later this afternoon."

"Of course—," Vega began, but he had already hung up.

"She was a German woman," Vega thought. She started the car and drove back toward Strasbourg. It was too early to pick up the kids, and the rain was still pouring down, so Vega went to the Patisserie Koenig in the Rue de Francs-Bourgeois for a croissant. But when she got there she could not bear just sitting there glaring at the wet faces and smelling the wet wool of the customers' coats. A blond woman in a gray raincoat walked in and sat down with her newspaper at a small round table next to Vega. Vega stared at her and saw the features of the dead girl in her mind: the makeup on the dead face was still intact, the high cheekbones jutting out, the face white and taut. Who had she been? What had she done here in Alsace? A model and a junkie in this small town? How had she ended up here, and finally, at the spring on Mont Ste Odile? Not for healing but to die.

Vega picked up a *Strasbourg Daily* and thumbed through it in search of an article about the murder. At first she overlooked it, it was so small. Just a short notice on page eight.

> *Young Woman Found Dead on Mont Ste Odile*
> *The body of a young woman has been found dead behind the Spring of Tears on Mont Ste. Odile. According to the authorities, the victim died between 2 and 4 AM early Tuesday morning. The police are following leads, which may connect the victim to a missing person who was registered at a boarding house by the Place du Temple Neuf. Please direct any information relating to this incident to the local police station in Hagenau.*

No mention of the missing eyes. No mention of the shoe. Maybe the police wanted to keep some details confidential to give them an edge in the investigation. The Rue de L'Outre by the Place du Temple Neuf was not far, and Vega had an umbrella. She could just walk by and see what kind of house the victim had lived in. You could tell a lot about a person by the way they live, she thought. Walking under her red umbrella in the pelting rain, she imagined the dead woman coming home this way, from shopping or from a job. There was a little tobacco shop at the corner. She would have stopped there for a pack of cigarettes. For some reason, Vega was sure that she had smoked. She continued on to the Place du Temple Neuf where she saw an old-fashioned sign whose paint was now peeling: *Pension Gluck, individual studios, and rooms for rent, weekly or monthly rates.* The building Rue du L'Outre Number 13 was a 1950s concrete structure that had seen better days, just as the dead woman had. Vega stood in the rain under her umbrella staring at the pension. It did not look like a particularly inviting place to come home to. The smoked-glass entrance door opened and a woman, who looked to be in her late fifties, wearing a flower-patterned housedress, stuck her head out.

"What are you staring at? Do you want a room? If not, then I suggest you move on!" the woman hissed.

"Me?" Vega looked around, but there was nobody else on the soaking wet sidewalk, "I am sorry, nothing's wrong, or actually yes, something is wrong. One of your guests. She used to live here. She died."

"The Parker girl? You a friend of Sarah Parker? Well, that's the first good news I've heard all day. Maybe you can pay the rent she owes me. Police was here and told me she's dead. So, now who's gonna take care of her debt? And they put yellow tape all over the studio. How am I supposed to rent it out like that? What if people find out she's been murdered? Nobody's gonna want to live in her space. 'How long are you gonna keep that tape there,' I ask. They just shake their heads, them policemen, and they don't care how regular peoples get by. They're just interested in their murder investigation. I coulda told them, she would come to a bad end, that girl. She was up to no good, I knew it. I seen enough people come through here, and I can tell. I should have never taken her in, but I had a vacancy. Now, what do you want, mademoiselle? I can't let you in, it's all taped off, and I'm not gonna get myself into trouble with the police, so . . ." The barrage of verbiage suddenly subsided as quickly as it had started.

" I am sorry Sarah Parker caused you so much aggravation," Vega interjected.

"I've seen worse. May her soul rest in peace, not like her body, which never seemed at peace at all!" came the answer suddenly in a much softer tone.

"Are all her things still here?" Vega asked timidly but encouraged by the more conciliatory tone.

"What do you mean, her stuff? She barely had anything. I coulda just packed it all in two cardboard boxes, and thrown it out, but the police wouldn't let me. They need to follow the leads, whatever that means. I coulda told them where to look, doesn't take a rocket scientist. She hung around with bad folks, so I am not surprised she ended up in a ditch!" Vega winced at the coarse words.

"I wish I could help . . ." she muttered.

"Well, it's too late for that now!" the landlady concluded and slammed the door in her face with a flourish. At that moment a lorry drove through a deep puddle and splashed dirty rainwater all over Vega's legs and skirt. Too late she jumped to the side. Wet like a soaked poodle she shook herself. Trotting back to her car she decided on an impulse to stop in the tobacco shop. At least it was warm and dry and smelled of pipe smoke, just like her grandfather's office used to smell. A slim man in corduroy pants and wire-rim glasses sat on a stool behind the counter and read a well-fingered manuscript. Behind him on the wall was a shelf packed with classic books of literature, from Moliere, Voltaire, Schiller, and Goethe, to Dostoyevsky and Kafka, which took up more space than the actual tobacco wares he carried. He glanced up at her and a smile crossed his face at her drooping wet appearance.

"Can I help you?" he asked. "Maybe with a towel?"

"Maybe," Vega began haltingly. "I don't smoke, but I have a question about one of your customers, or at least I assume she was your customer . . ." she faltered.

"Ah, madame, I am like a priest. The secrets of my customers are safe with me to the grave."

"My question extends beyond the grave. The customer I am talking about is dead." His head suddenly snapped to attention and his eyes looked at her piercingly.

"Continue, madame, who are you talking about?"

"Sarah Parker. Blond, in her thirties, high cheekbones—"

"Yes, yes, of course I know Mademoiselle Parker. You say she is dead?"

"Murdered it seems. Three days ago."

"*Mon Dieu*, was that why the police were here this morning? I knew her quite well; she came here almost every day. She smoked Camel Filters. At least a pack a day. Sometimes we talked. She borrowed a few of my books. Several customers do. It brings them back, and we talk about the plots."

"Which books did she borrow?"

"It may be significant, no? She liked Dostoyevsky, *Crime and Punishment*. I remember she said, even if you don't believe in a god, your sins will haunt you and your victims for a lifetime. At the time I wondered what haunted her. She always seemed on edge, as if she was on the run from something. Actually, she never returned my copy of *Crime and Punishment* . . ." He turned around and pointed at an empty slot on his shelf.

"I liked her. Once or twice we had coffee together," he continued. "This is terrible news. I must admit, I am a little shaken. I think I'll close down shop for a while. I need to digest that she is gone. Would you have a cup of coffee with me at the corner bistro?"

"Only if I am not intruding."

"Of course not. Did you know her?"

"No, I found her, or actually I found her shoe."

"She always wore beautiful shoes, Sarah did," said the storeowner as he stuck in the window a well-used-looking sign that announced, "*Je reviens en cinq minutes.*"

Like the rest of the neighborhood, the corner bistro was very simple and small, with only five round tables surrounded by wicker chairs. They sat down by the rain-streaked window, and Vega ordered her third *café au lait* this morning. Jean Bonnard, as he introduced himself, reminisced about Sarah.

"There was something mysterious about her. I felt she had a dark secret. She was not taking care of herself very well, and on some days she looked like hell, pale and drawn and twitching. I was pretty sure she was doing drugs. Other days she looked good. She could really pull herself together, great makeup and clothes. She gave guided tours of Strasbourg for German tourists. Or maybe it was more like an escort service. In any case she knew quite a bit about the city and its history. I gave her some books about the cathedral and the astronomical clock. She liked it here. She said it felt small and safe, which sadly for her turned out not to be true. Sometimes I wouldn't see her for days, and I'd worry about her, but then she'd appear again, either looking up or really down. It was always either one or the other with Sarah."

"Did she have friends?" Vega dared to ask.

"I don't know. I don't think so. She'd only been here for a short time, and I don't think she had many visitors. But Madame Gluck, the landlady, would know about that."

"I already made the acquaintance of Madame Gluck," Vega said and grimaced. Jean laughed.

"She is quite formidable, isn't she?" he asked. Vega realized that she quite enjoyed sitting and talking with this thoughtful young man when a sudden glance to her watch made her jump up in a panic.

"My children—excuse me—I have to pick them up now." And she ran out into the rain again.

Wednesday, May 13, Klingenthal, 4 PM:

In the afternoon, Vega sat at the kitchen table, a towel wrapped around her wet hair, arranging the pictures from Mont Ste Odile, including the photo of the pink shoe on the table in front of her. She tried to decide which ones to use in her article. Stevie sat next to her doing his math homework.

"Mom, listen to this: There are twelve children in line at the snack bar. Four children are in front of Sandy. How many children are behind her? What do you think?"

"It does not matter what I think, Stevie, we should just figure out exactly what the number is, right? How about you draw a little picture, Stevie? Here, this line is the snack bar, and then we put the children in front, okay?"

"Okay, okay, let me do it!" Stevie eagerly grabbed the paper and started drawing with much concentration, the tip of his tongue sticking out of his mouth. The doorbell rang. Vega looked out the window into the still pelting rain and wondered who would visit on such a day. She fingered her towel, but then sighed, resigned to her rather undignified appearance, and opened the door, where she found a soaking wet M. Bonacourt.

"Inspector, please come inside, out of this nasty weather. Excuse my towel, but I got pretty soaked this morning."

"Madame, I apologize for intruding, but I wanted to pick up the picture of the shoe *in situ*." Taking his coat and umbrella, Vega watched the inspector progress into the living room, leaving small water puddles on the floor in his wake.

"Would you like some tea? Coffee?" she asked.

"I would love a cup of coffee, thank you very much."

"This is my son Steven. Stevie, this is Monsieur Bonacourt from the police. He solves many crimes"

"Bonjour, inspector. Can you help me solve a really difficult math problem?"

Laughing they continued into the kitchen, but Stevie was not amused. While Vega prepared coffee, the inspector leaned against the kitchen counter and studied the many colorful artworks covering every inch of the refrigerator surface.

"Here is the photo of the location where I found the shoe." Vega grabbed the picture from the table and handed it to the inspector, who studied it carefully.

"Is this exactly where and how you found the shoe?" he asked.

"Yes, and when I studied the picture, I noticed the position of the shoe. It almost looks like a pink arrow, pointing in the direction of the body. Almost as if the murderer wanted to give us a hint, a message." Vega looked over his shoulder.

"An interesting observation. I wonder if it was intended that way."

"You know of course that at the Spring of Tears Ste Odile gained her eyesight, while the victim lost hers. A strange contrast, wouldn't you say?" Vega observed, while grinding the coffee beans in an old-fashioned hand-operated coffee mill.

"We might get a little bit ahead of ourselves with this interpretation," cautioned the inspector. "But I will keep it in mind." Vega put the kettle on and placed the filter on top of the white coffee pot.

"What is going to happen next?" Vega asked.

"The victim had a brother in Germany," the inspector said, "He is a philosophy professor in Tübingen. He has been notified by the local authorities and is coming to formally identify the body. We will interview him in Hagenau about his relationship with his sister. He does not speak French, and very little English. Since I do not speak German, we will use a translator."

"Inspector, please let me attend the interview. I could listen not only to his words, but his intonation, read between the lines. Was he close to his sister? Does he know anything, he is not telling us?" pleaded Vega, while pouring coffee and steaming milk into white ceramic cups with slightly shaky hands.

"Excellent café au lait, madame," said the inspector, taking a sip to gain some time while considering her suggestion. Vega smiled, thinking that this was her fourth cup this day.

"Did her autopsy reveal anything?" she asked.

"The autopsy results show that the victim died around three o'clock on Monday morning. She had a very high dose of heroin in her blood, but probably not enough to kill her. She was a regular user and had a high tolerance for the drug. In addition she had abrasions on the back of her head and legs. They could have resulted from dragging her behind the spring, but the pathologist thinks that her eyes were cut out before her body was moved and could have been the cause of death."

"She was blinded while she was still alive?" Vega gasped.

"Basically yes." Both of them were silent for a moment, and the only sounds in the room were pelting rain and Stevie's scratching pencil. Vega hoped Stevie had not heard the last words they had spoken.

"Well, I think that's all. Thank you for the coffee, madame." Bonacourt got up.

Vega felt panic inside. She could not just let him leave.

"Who was she? Who was the victim?"

"That's what we have to find out."

"Please let me help you, inspector," Vega pleaded, wondering about the urgency she felt. "Let me attend the interview."

"Why would you want to do that?"

"I think it could be helpful if I met Sarah Parker's brother."

"How did you know her name was Sarah Parker," Bonacourt asked sharply. Vega blushed.

"I spoke to her landlady," she admitted.

"How did you find her landlady?"

"I read the notice about the murder in the *Strasbourg Daily*. It mentioned the location of the boarding house. Is there a reason why her name is kept private?"

"Until her brother has officially identified her, we are just assuming her name was Sarah Parker. What else do you know about her?"

"I don't know anything, but I could read between the lines of the interview."

"It is out of the question, it would be highly unprofessional," the inspector sighed. "Why are you so interested in Sarah Parker?"

"I ask myself the same question. I guess, I feel somehow responsible, because I found her."

"Don't become too interested. It might make you a suspect," Bonacourt warned.

"In that case it is in your interest to keep an eye on me and my reactions," Vega suggested.

"I could not justify to my colleagues why you were tagging along."

"You could tell them that I was a friend of the victim, which is kind of true, except that I only met her after she died." Vega argued.

"At this point I need to know as much as possible about Sarah Parker's life. What was she involved in? Who had cause to harm her? I guess you could observe the interview from the adjoining room through the one-way mirror," he finally relented.

"Inspector, thank you. I really appreciate your trust. You won't regret this. No wonder Madame Merrier thinks so highly of you." The inspector smiled modestly.

"The interview is scheduled for Saturday afternoon at three o'clock. Come to the precinct in Hagenau."

"I'll be there."

Vega walked Bonacourt to the door and then returned to the dining room table.

"How is the math homework going, Stevie?"

"Very well; see here are the children in front of the snack bar. This is Arno, he is first in line. He looks like a caterpillar and his body is all covered with tiny green poisonous spikes. Then comes little Jack-in-the-Box, he makes a scary face because he just popped out of the box. After him comes a little robot guy, but his body parts got mixed up and now his leg is coming out of the shoulder …"

"Stevie! You don't need to tell me the life story of all the kids in line! Can you just count how many are behind Sandy?"

"I did not get that far yet. Here is Sandy; she is really skinny and her mom gave her a Euro for a snack, but she dropped it and now she is crawling around on the floor looking for it—"

"Now look Stevie, this is all very interesting, but how many kids are standing in line behind Sandy?"

"I just finished three of them. Mom, it takes a long time, because this kid looks like an X and this one fell down, or actually he wants to lie on the floor so the other kids trip over him—"

"Stevie, can I ask you a question?"

45

"Of course, Mom, anytime."

"Does the snack line at your school look like this?"

"Of course not. There are a lot more children than this at my school. You want me to draw them for you?"

"No thank you. I think we just finish this line here. Do you mind if I just draw a few more kids so we have twelve altogether and then we can count the ones behind Sandy? We'll just draw them plainly like this, okay?"

"I am sorry, Mom, but they look much too simple. No child is that simple."

To which, of course, Vega had to agree.

Saturday, May 16, 3 PM, Hagenau Precinct:

When Vega entered the one-way mirror room at the precinct, the inspector, the translator, and Sarah's brother, Karl, were already in the adjoining interview room, which looked sterile and grim, with institutional green washable paint on the walls and small, barred windows close to the ceiling.

"Dr. Parker, have you identified the body?" asked Inspector Bonacourt through the translator.

Karl Parker sat across the bare wooden table from them. He looked very pale and his eyes lay in deep hollow sockets. He nodded gravely.

"Dr. Parker, please state for the record that you have identified the body of your sister, Sarah Parker."

"I have identified the body of my sister Sarah Parker," he repeated obediently.

"When did you last see your sister?"

"She came to visit us in Tübingen, two weekends ago. She spent Saturday and Sunday with my family at our home."

"How did she seem at the time? Was she well? Nervous? Did she talk about something troubling her?"

"Something always troubled Sarah. She did not seem worse than usual. She played a lot with my daughter, Rachel, whom she adores, I mean adored.

Rachel is the main reason Sarah moved to Strasbourg. She wanted to be near her. The two were inseparable when they were together. I don't know how to explain this to Rachel." He buried his face in his hands.

"How old is Rachel?"

"Rachel is four. She loved her aunt. She thought she was the most beautiful woman on earth. When Sarah was around Rachel, she became a different person. She suddenly became funny and tender and very protective."

"What did your sister do for a living?" The inspector changed the subject, but Vega wanted to hear more about Rachel. She felt that this relationship between aunt and niece was important.

"Sarah did the odd modeling job. She used to be good and made quite a lot of money once, but she had some personal problems and lately she mostly led guided tours, I think. City tours for German tourists." Vega thought about the escort-service angle Jean, the tobacconist, had mentioned.

"Did you know any of her friends here in Strasbourg?" Bonacourt asked.

"I don't think she had any friends. My sister was not a social person. She stayed to herself."

"Did you ever visit her here?"

"Yes, we came once in a while. We would pick her up and spend the day in the country, on the *route du vin*, eating lunch in country inns and taking walks. We never stayed over night. We live less than two hours by car from here."

"Have you been to the pension where she lived?" Bonacourt asked.

Karl sighed. "She usually lived in places like that. I offered to help her with the rent, asked her if she wanted to move into an apartment, but she seemed to prefer living in places she could leave at a moment's notice."

"Why is that, in your opinion?"

"I don't know. And believe me it is not for lack of trying to find out. She was scared of someone following her. For years Sarah moved from one dingy hotel to another; from one city to the next."

"Why didn't she live with you, or at least close by, if your daughter was so important to her?"

"She said she could never live in Germany again, and Strasbourg was as close as she would go. Again, I could not figure out why, and she did not explain it to me. My sister did many irrational things. Sometimes I thought it was just a paranoia she had, but I am not a psychologist."

"Did she ever see a psychologist or a psychiatrist?"

"I think she went for a while, when she lived in New York. But it did not seem to make much of a difference in her behavior."

"When did she leave New York?"

"About four years ago, just before I got married. After New York she traveled in India and then came here."

"Were you close to your sister?"

"As close as you could get. She never let you get really close. There was a definite barrier, except with Rachel. But she always stayed in touch with me. I always knew where she was and what she was doing." There it was again; the little girl Rachel was very important, thought Vega.

"Do you have any other relatives?"

"No, we are the entire family. Our parents have been dead for years. There are a few cousins around, but we don't have any contact with them. It was just the two of us. We were the black sheep of the family because of some old family scandal. Nobody wanted to have anything to do with us."

"Would anybody from your family have reason to cause your sister any harm?"

Karl stared incredulously at the inspector.

"Sarah was no threat to anybody. If anything she was a threat to herself. Why would anyone want to hurt her? Our family just ignored us, they did not hate us. We didn't do anything to them. Something happened before my father died. Many families have rifts like that. It doesn't mean they kill each other."

"I am sorry, Dr Parker, I did not want to imply anything. We are just looking into all possibilities. You knew your sister best, so we rely on you."

"Yes, I understand you are doing your job. I just can't accept the fact that she is dead, and that somebody killed her!"

"I realize how difficult this must be for you. Please answer just one more question for us: How did you contact your sister?"

"I called her cell phone, of course."

"We need that number and carrier to check her phone records. Her phone was not part of her belongings anymore when we found her."

"Whoever killed her stole the phone?" Karl asked.

"Apparently."

"Here is the number; I hope her phone records give you some clues."

"We'll do our best," concluded the inspector, "and please let us know if you can think of anything else that could help understand what happened. Anything she said, any people she may have mentioned!"

The inspector rose and shook hands with Karl, who walked out of the room with sunken shoulders and a hanging head.

"Herr Parker!" Vega hurried after Karl, as he made his way down the precinct hallway.

"Yes?" he turned around warily and Vega saw the tiredness and the big, dark circles under his eyes.

"I don't want to bother you," she said in German. "My name is Vega Stern, and I just wanted to tell you how very, very sorry I am that this had to happen to your sister."

"Who are you? Did you know my sister?" Parker asked.

"I found her, or actually I found her shoe at the Spring of Tears. I can barely imagine how terrible this must be for you. You seem to have been very close to her."

He looked almost grateful.

"Thank you for acknowledging that she was a human being. It seems that everybody is talking about Sarah, as if she was an item, case #13B187. She was a beautiful and mysterious young woman. But when I saw her on the metal slab in the morgue, where I had to identify her, she looked like an object. There was no color, no life left in her."

Vega remembered the headshot of the dead woman, as pale and still as a marble statue.

"It must have been a terrible shock," she mumbled.

"I suddenly realized that all these people here, the inspector and the police, they never knew her alive. They only know her like this, as a dead piece of flesh, and so it is no wonder they treat her as such in their minds and in their attitude."

"I know Monsieur Bonacourt is doing his best," Vega interjected gently.

"I know, but he cannot bring her back. I just cannot get over the fact that this is all that's left of her." Karl was not to be consoled. Not yet, not for a long time maybe.

"Her things," Vega suddenly remembered. "The police will release her belongings on Monday or Tuesday and I am going to visit my mother in the Black Forest early next week. I can bring them to you, if you like."

"Would you? That is very kind, and it is a little less impersonal than a police delivery. I live in Tübingen. It's not very far."

"I know. I used to study art history there."

"You know it very well then. We philosophers share a building with the art historians. But of course you know that."

Vega nodded. "Just let the police know that I will bring your sister's belongings, and I'll be there on Monday or Tuesday."

"Thank you." He shook Vega's hand and continued walking down the stairs.

"Why am I doing this?" thought Vega immediately. "Why am I getting involved, volunteering to do the police's job?" "It makes Karl feel better," said a little voice in the back of her head. "It satisfies your curiosity," said another voice, from a different corner of her mind.

"Shut up," mumbled Vega.

"Excuse me madame, are you talking to me?" The inspector stood next to her with a grin on his face.

"Inspector, I need to talk to you."

"Certainly. We can talk in my office."

Inspector Bonacourt's office was like its occupant, slightly disheveled. It had piles of papers on the wooden chairs and a desk completely covered with files and reference books. Amongst them Vega spotted a Gourmet magazine, a novel by Victor Hugo, and a volume of essays by Voltaire.

"Please take a seat, madame," offered the inspector, while moving piles of paper from one chair to another. "What did you think of the brother?"

"I think he is sincere. I think he truly is in shock and his grief is real. It seems to me that the little girl, Rachel, his daughter, could be a clue to Sarah's mystery."

"In which regard?" the inspector asked with interest.

"Sarah Parker seemed to project a lot of herself into that little girl."

"What makes you say that, madame?"

"Just a gut feeling, an intuition. You believe in them, don't you?" The inspector raised his eyebrows, so Vega continued,

"I also found out that Sarah did have a friend, of sorts."

"How did you happen to find that out, madame?"

"He is the owner of the tobacco store next to the pension where Sarah lived, and she saw him almost every day to buy her Camel Filters. They started talking; he also runs a little lending library out of his shop, and Sarah borrowed books from him and then they talked about them after she had read them. His name is Jean, and you might enjoy talking to him. He seems quite knowledgeable about Voltaire and Hugo." Vega blushed slightly, as she nodded toward the French classics among the inspector's volumes. I might as well get it over with, she thought, and barreled on.

"And her landlady says that she knew Sarah would come to a bad ending, and she could point the police in the direction of the bad company Sarah kept. She is quite a formidable character."

"Madame, are you here to negotiate a police consultant's fee, or are you trying to do our job for us?"

"I am sorry, I did not mean to interfere, it just so happened that —"

" — that you stumbled into the victim's lodging address and landlady and friends. Anything else you would like to tell me about?"

"No, that's all, except that Dr. Parker asked me to bring him Sarah's belongings when they are released, and that's about it."

The inspector suddenly erupted into laughter; his face twitched and his mustache quivered as he roared unrestrainedly. Vega watched him for a minute, and then joined in, relieved at this turn of events.

"Madame, I could not pay you if I tried," he finally managed to say, "and I know better than to stand in the way of a woman with a mission. Bitter experience with my former wife has taught me a lesson or two. By all means, after he confirms his consent, take the belongings of the victim to her brother. They will be released on Monday. You can pick them up here. Visit with him. Maybe you find out more about the connection with little Rachel. I never underestimate female intuition. In regard to M. Jean from the tobacco shop, I will follow up and probe his knowledge of the classics. But be careful, madame. A murder investigation is not to be trifled with."

Vega drove home to Klingenthal feeling very cheerful. On the way she stopped to pick up corned beef and cabbage, as well as a fresh baguette and an apple tart from her local baker. Her husband Greg had come back from Ireland, and they improvised an Irish feast to celebrate his return. She thought about the proper wine to match the meal, but concluded that it probably would have to be Irish whiskey. The meal was a great success; they listened to the Irish folk music Greg had brought back, and Stevie entertained them with some innovative dance moves. Daniel shared his knowledge of Irish Druids and Celtic mythological creatures, and Vega was happy to contribute that the Pagan Wall surrounding Mont Ste Odile was probably of Celtic origin and included cup stones in the Druids grotto, just like those found in ancient Celtic sites. Suddenly the family was interested in taking a walk with her along the wall to the Druids grotto the very next day.

Sunday, May 17, Klingenthal, 10 AM:

At breakfast on Sunday morning Stevie, his cheeks full of pancakes asked, "How many pancakes can God eat?"

Vega and her husband grinned at each other. Stevie always came up with the most puzzling questions during meals, especially if he could not finish his plate and wanted to distract his parents.

"That's a tough question," Greg finally concluded.

"I bet he could eat a hundred or more," Stevie guessed.

"He probably could, but I don't think God needs to eat pancakes. He does not have a body like you and me."

"He has one thousand arms though, doesn't he? You showed me a picture of him just last week," intercepted Daniel, looking at Vega accusingly.

"There is a Tibetan Buddhist god that has one thousand arms, that's correct. His name is Avalokiteshvara."

"That's a very long name. It must be hard to remember for the people who pray to him," observed Stevie pragmatically.

"Why does he have so many arms?" Daniel pursued.

"So he can help more people all at the same time, because he is the god of compassion. He also has eleven heads, so he can see better who needs him."

"He could eat eleven pancakes all at once, and hold one thousand extras in each hand!" was Stevie's very logical conclusion.

During their walk along the Pagan Wall, Mona jumped excitedly in front of everybody's feet, and the boys pretended to shoot bows and arrows at each other from opposite sides of the wall. Vega told her husband about the pink shoe and the events it had set into motion. He immediately agreed to take care of the boys for a day so she could go to Tübingen and visit her mother in Germany.

"I know this is all very exciting, but be careful!" he warned. "What are they all thinking," Vega wondered, "that the killer is coming after me next?"

On their way home they stopped for a voluminous lunch at the *Golden Swan,* under the watchful eye of Mme. Merrier, who stopped by their table frequently and had a hard time restraining her curiosity about the progress of the murder investigation. By the time they reached home everyone felt content and sleepy. The afternoon was warm and golden, and Daniel swung gently in the hammock on the porch, while Greg and Stevie took a nap together. Vega sat at the garden table outside, trying to work on her article. She looked out over the lime green vines and the blooming fruit trees toward the village and felt very fortunate. She had so much to be grateful for: two precious sons, a kind husband, a beautiful house to live in, a bellyful of delicious Alsatian food, and the freedom to determine her life as she wished. In contrast, Sarah had possessed so little: no friends to speak of, belongings that fit into two cardboard boxes, a dingy rented room, a life spent on the run from real or imagined demons.

"Mom?"

"Yes, Danny?"

"Do we believe in God?"

"Sure, we believe in gods. You children were gifts from the gods. We just don't give the gods specific names, so as not to offend others."

"Is Jesus a god?"

"You know that Christians consider him the son of God."

"He is a semi-god then," said Daniel, "because his mother was human. Kind of like Hercules, who had a god for a father, but a mortal mother."

"I suppose you could say that, even though I think most Christians would not agree."

"Why not?"

"They would not like the comparison with the Greek gods, because they consider them pagan, plus they would say Jesus is a full-fledged god."

"So that means Christians have more than one god."

"They would not agree with that either."

"That does not make sense then, unless Mary was a goddess as well."

"Well, you're right, religion is often irrational. They ask you to believe certain things, even if they do not make sense."

"Can gods count to infinity?" Daniel had pursued his quest for infinity since he was three years old and could count to ten.

"Probably, they have all the time in the world. But I would hope they have something better to do than count to infinity, because they would never get done."

Daniel looked disappointed, but then his face lightened up.

"It would be very discouraging, if poor people prayed to the gods for help and they could not answer, because they were counting to infinity and therefore needed to concentrate on their numbers instead of the people's prayers."

"That would really be a shame and very discouraging," agreed Vega.

"But sometimes I think maybe that's exactly what's happening, because the gods don't seem to answer a lot of prayers, exactly."

Vega could not think of any counter argument to that, so she let it go. But the image of a whole group of gods sitting around and counting to infinity since the beginning of time, and waving away the pleas of humans as inconvenient, lodged itself into her mind.

Monday, May 18, Strasbourg:

Before fetching the boys from school, Vega picked up Sarah's belongings from the precinct at Hagenau. As predicted, they consisted merely of a suitcase and one cardboard box with odds and ends sticking out. The officer on duty made her sign an inventory list to be co-signed by Karl and then returned to the police.

"They found no fingerprints in her room, I guess?" she asked the uniformed officer, who helped her carry the objects to the car.

"Madame, they found more fingerprints than they could count. That place hadn't been cleaned in at least two years. There were layers of fingerprints, some surely belonging to people, who don't even walk this earth anymore."

Vega smiled at his indignation, and her opinion of Sarah's lodging choice sank even lower than it had been.

The officer helped her load the suitcase into the trunk and the box onto the backseat of her car. On the way home Stevie had to sit next to it, while Daniel occupied the front seat.

"Mom, what is all that stuff?" Stevie asked.

"I have to take it to Germany when I visit your grandma tomorrow. It belonged to a dead person."

"Creepy! Is her ghost hidden in this box?"

"I hope not."

"It depends on how the person died. Did she die normally, Mom?"

"She didn't. Actually she was killed!"

"Super-creepy!" they both exclaimed.

"Mom, in that case her ghost is definitely still hovering around. She'll probably haunt this car now for a few years to come," announced Stevie with much authority.

"What makes you say that? Since when are you such an expert on ghosts?"

"Mom, you know I believe in ghosts, plus I know about these things from my invisible friends."

"Yes, how are they, by the way?"

"Good. Josh moved out, but Bob is still here."

"Are Bob and Josh ghosts?"

"No, of course not. They are just invisible."

"But they tell you about ghosts?"

"Well, some of their friends are ghosts, but not mine."

Fortunately, at this complicated moment in the conversation they reached the house and the boys jumped out and ran up the driveway with Mona.

Looking through Sarah's belongings in her bedroom, Vega's heart beat loudly. She felt like an intruder, violating the dead woman's privacy, and probably she was breaking some sort of confidentiality agreement as well. The suitcase was sealed with yellow crime scene tape, so she left it in the trunk of her car, but the box was open on top. It contained the expected odds and ends:

- One small pillow in a yellow pillowcase (probably from an airplane)
- A photograph of Karl and Rachel in a silver picture frame; they stood in a park in front of playground equipment on a gray day. Rachel was

holding Karl's hand. Her face was very pale and white, hardly contrasting the light blond curls framing her small and smiling features. She wore bright yellow rubber boots and a pink raincoat with orange mittens

- A half-wilted kind of spider plant, a hardy species, but showing serious signs of neglect
- A half-eaten box of Lindt nougat chocolates

Vega shuddered seeing this box. It suddenly made the death of this young woman so tangible. She imagined Sarah taking out the last piece of chocolate of her life, eating it and expecting to have the rest later, when she came back. Except there was no later and she never came back to her room.

- A portable CD player with several CDs ranging from Bach to U2.
- Five books, among them Nietzsche's *Thus Spoke Zarathustra* and Dostoyevsky's *Crime and Punishment*, (Vega made a mental note to tell Karl that the Dostoyevsky belonged to Jean the tobacconist) as well as Hermann Hesse's *Siddharta*

As Vega fingered the books, a photograph fell out of the Nietzsche book: It showed another little girl and her father. The photograph was black and white and the clothes of the child and man indicated that it was probably taken in the sixties. The little girl was blond as well, and she was looking up at her father, who wore a double-breasted suit and a hat. In one hand he held a cigarette, in the other his daughter's small hand. He was smiling at the camera, a proud and tender smile, while the girl looking up at him, was equally proud. Her small legs were dressed in white knee-high socks and black lacquer shoes. Vega could tell by looking at the picture that the two were very close and devoted to each other. "Little Sarah and her father," she thought and put the picture back into the book for Karl. Next she found

- A cigarette lighter

- A candle
- A half-smoked pack of Camel cigarettes
- An ashtray with the logo of a beer brand on its side

There was also

- A fashion magazine (Vogue) and
- A red-white-and-blue coffee mug

The final item in the cardboard box was:

- A scroll of some kind, rolled up around a wooden dowel.

Vega carefully unraveled the scroll and revealed a canvas painting surrounded by a blue brocade frame. She recognized it as Asian, but her training was in Western art and she was not sure of its precise origin and purpose. This last item was such a departure from the rest of Sarah's sad collection of odds and ends that it seemed to belong to a different person. It was a work of art, a painting of some value and significance, of that Vega was sure. In mind-boggling detail and confusing abundance it depicted a large circle, or wheel, held in the clutches of a demonic red-skinned monster with a skull crown on its grotesque head. The wheel itself was subdivided into six sections, and each section was populated by a host of bizarre and strange creatures. Some looked like animals, others like giants; still others had deformed and ghostly white bodies with endlessly long necks and inflated bellies. In one section the creatures seemed to burn in fires and were tortured by small demons. The topmost section showed a pleasant and luxurious scene, where the miniscule humanoids lounged and listened to divine music under shady groves in fragrant gardens.

Vega had to blink at this visual onslaught. Her eyes searched for a place to rest, but every square inch of the canvas was covered with elaborate detail and colorful paint. The center of the circle consisted of three animals, a pig, a snake and a rooster, biting each other's tails. The next concentric circle around them showed an ascending row of people dressed in maroon robes and a descending row of screaming and terrified creatures plunging into utter despair. The outside of the wheel, surrounding the six main sections consisted again of a narrow ring with a parade of people, animals, trees, and symbols. Behind the red, grinning monster, holding the circle in his claws, stretched an unfamiliar landscape with pointy blue and white mountains, arabesque clouds, and cascading rivers in emerald green pastures. Gods or demons floated in the sky and underneath the wheel.

"Holy cow," muttered Vega, "this is way out of my league." She had never seen anything like this, and was simultaneously repulsed and fascinated by the images. Could this jumble of strange images harbor a key to Sarah's life? Why did Sarah, who traveled so lightly, carry it with her so faithfully, from one dwelling place to another, one city, one country, to the next? At this moment the bedroom door flew open and Stevie burst in, throwing himself belly first onto the bed.

"Hi Mom, find any ghosts?" he asked cheerfully.

"Yeah, I think so," Vega responded hesitantly.

"Told you! I knew there where ghosts in that box. Just don't keep them in the house overnight, okay?"

"Alright, fine. Let me just take a picture of this."

"What is it? Oh, that's creepy!"

"A little bit, I agree."

"By the way, Danny and I are hungry."

Vega took a picture of the strange painting and turned it around to roll it back up, when she saw a vertical row of unfamiliar letters and symbols running down the middle. With her finger she traced what she assumed to be a blessing or a spell down to the blue brocade border, which formed a sort of pocket on the backside of the painting. She pushed aside the fabric border to see where the inscription ended and she heard a faint rustling sound, like cellophane. She pushed back the fabric further and found a hidden pocket, secured by rows of fine stitches on three sides, behind the brocade border. Probing with her pinky finger she discovered a flat object stuck there in the very corner completely covered by the blue brocade. Carefully, Vega kept the brocade border pulled aside and pulled the object out of its pocket. It turned out to be a picture in a plastic cover attached to the canvas backing. Vega pried it loose and turned it around. It was another old black and white print with a white jagged border. Two young men smiled at her from a different time. Their arms were around each other's shoulders. Their hair was parted and slicked back orderly in good 1950s fashion. One of them wore a V-neck sweater with a diamond pattern and a white shirt and tie underneath. The other wore a priest's collar. Vega detected a slight resemblance in their faces and guessed that they could be relatives. Both had blond hair and high cheekbones. The man with the priest collar had a mole on his forehead, above his left brow. Vega saw nothing unusual or suspicious in their smiling expressions that would explain the carefully concealed location of the picture. "They look harmless enough," Vega thought. The picture seemed to be taken in a living room, in front of a sofa, and Vega could discern a painting on the wall behind the pair. She noticed shapes resembling building blocks painted in a childlike fashion in the background. There was a bright round shape floating on top and the texture looked quite sophisticated, despite the naïve appearance. The style looked familiar to Vega, but she could not pinpoint in what way.

"Mom, when is dinner ready?" sounded Stevie's squeaky voice up from the first floor.

"Just a minute, sweetheart." She took a picture of the photo then replaced it exactly where she had found it, and finally returned to her motherly duties.

Tuesday, May 19, Autobahn A5, Direction Karlsruhe

The box with Sarah's belongings on the backseat, scroll sticking out, the kids and Mona safely in the care of her husband, a picture of the ghostly painting in her camera, Vega drove at 180 km/h through the dense Black Forest, which stood darkly on either side of the Autobahn. She knew this route by heart. Her thoughts wandered back to the strange Asian painting and its myriad tiny creatures writhing in their separate sections unable to reach out or touch each other. Which of the sections had Sarah inhabited? Certainly not the same sphere as Vega and her family. All she knew so far about Sarah made Vega believe that she had existed in a dark and tormented place where it was almost impossible to reach her, where even her own brother had been unable to access her thoughts and feelings. Having arrived at this sad conclusion, Vega's mind traveled ahead to her immediate destination: Tübingen, to talk to Karl, maybe find out more about Rachel and Sarah's relationship. But before that she would visit her own mother, a task that filled her with dread.

An hour and a half later, Vega stood at the entrance gate of St. Sophie's, her mother's Catholic nursing home. The day was pleasant and sunny. Daffodils swayed in a mild breeze in planters surrounding a softly gurgling fountain. Old women sat at tables in wheelchairs and held their faces up into the sun.

Some had company; others sat alone. An old man in his wheelchair sat apart from the others scrutinizing the visitor. He squinted suspiciously. Vega noticed that he wore a priest's collar and wrapped around his hands, resting in his lap, was a wooden rosary. But he did not move the beads between his fingers, and his mind did not seem to focus on prayer as he shot Vega a nasty look. Vega passed him nodding, smiling, and murmuring *"Guten Tag!"* as friendly as she could manage. She entered the building and climbed the stairs to the third floor, passing nurses in white coats and patients on benches and armchairs in the hallway. The nuns and Catholic lay staff, who ran the center, considered their care for the elderly a labor of love, and tried to nurture both their bodies and souls. As Vega entered Room 307, she saw her mother in the wheelchair, facing the window, her back to the door.

"Mom, how are you?" Vega said and kissed her cheek. Her mother's head was bent far to the right side, a trickle of saliva drooled out of the corner of her mouth. Vega wiped it off.

"Do you want to go outside? It is beautiful today." Without waiting for an answer she knew would not come, Vega continued talking.

"Let's go for a little walk, you will like it. It's warm and the flowers are blooming."

Her mother grunted something unintelligible, not directed at Vega. She had Parkinson's disease in the advanced stages and could not speak anymore. Communication was further hindered by the fact that her mother was unable to look at her directly. Her gaze was permanently fixed to the side and down. She could not lift her head. Vega loosened the brake, turned the chair around, laid a light shawl over her mother's shoulders, and pushed her to the elevator. As they rolled along the garden paths, Vega thought again, as she often did, how similar this was to pushing a baby stroller. When Stevie was a baby, she had pushed him for hours, talking to him aimlessly. He had sat in his seat, listening and making occasional comments such as:

"Grumbla. Blab," which Vega took as agreement. Now her mother was making similar noises, though Vega was not sure they had anything to do with her babbling narrative or with this present moment. Two years ago, when her mother's speech was still more understandable, they had often sat in this garden together, eating ice cream, and her mother had told her about the chickens, the goats, and most of all the cats that inhabited her world, though they were invisible to others. Once the three holy kings even crossed this very path, much to her mother's delight. In a conspiratorial voice she had told Vega that she had had a rendezvous with Vega's father at the fountain the night before. Vega had nodded confidentially, without mentioning that her father had been dead for twenty years, and that, even before his death, he had been married to a woman other than her mother. On a particularly good day Vega's mother had told her about Vega.

"You know what Vega is doing these days?" she asked in a gossipy tone.

"What?" Vega prompted.

"You won't believe what she's up to. She's become an astronaut and she is going into space!" she explained triumphantly. Vega was taken aback. As a child, she had always wanted to become the first German woman astronaut.

"Mother, but I am Vega!" she had said.

Her mother had looked at her confused, disbelieving, and angry. Vega immediately regretted her intrusion and the contradiction of her mother's daydream and had tried to assure her that all was fine. Nowadays even these little surreal exchanges had become impossible. Most days Vega doubted that her mother even knew that she was there. She had retreated into her own world completely and there was very little overlap, if any, with Vega's world or anybody else's world for that matter. The tentative connecting string to the outside had been cut and her mother now floated along in her own bubble, unencumbered by space or time. Maybe she was reliving her past, or creating a better world of her own liking. Vega hoped so. At least she did not seem unhappy, and once, when she was still more articulate, her mother had told Vega that she thought they had made a smart move by buying this vacation condominium, for which she obviously took the nursing home.

After the walk, Vega fed her mother some strawberries she had brought, kissed her on the cheek again, made sure she was comfortable, and left her in her room. When she descended the stairs, she took deep breaths of relief, grateful that she was able to leave this place. Many inhabitants spent the last thirty years of their lives right here, never even leaving the premises. On the way out she passed the priest again, but she did not slow down. She felt free, at least for a few moments of her obligation to her mother and free to just leave behind the stale smell of the home, and drive away without telling anybody where she was going.

It was lunchtime and Vega stopped at her favorite garden restaurant in the forest, right on the road to Tübingen. She had to walk the last three hundred meters since cars where not allowed on the forest paths. The light filtered through the fresh, lime green beech leaves and dappled the ground in front of her. The soil smelled deliciously fertile and full of the potential for ripening blackberries and wildflowers. Vega had been here with her mother and children many times. Her mother would never see this springtime forest again, but maybe it was so firmly embedded in her mind that she could recall it easily. Vega stretched her legs under the wooden bench and table on the grass in front of the *Gaststube*. She ate a sandwich with black forest ham and drank a cup of coffee. The sun felt warm on her back and the wild spring flowers lifted their little heads eagerly. In one day, she thought, how many feelings travel through us! Relief, regret, guilt, nostalgia, contentment, dread, impatience, pleasure, relief - all in the course of a few hours! She let go of the memory of her mother and enjoyed the moment.

Tuesday, May 19, Schönbuch Forest, 2:30 PM:

Vega took the small back roads through the Schönbuch forest to Tübingen. She passed through cut-your-own-flower-fields and through small villages with names like Waldenbuch und Dettenhausen. She passed the medieval monastery Bebenhausen and entered the old university town Tübingen in the early afternoon. She had to park the car in a lot on the outskirts of town, because the narrow medieval cobblestone streets were not constructed for car traffic. It was a good day for a stroll and Vega had taken this walk so many times as a student that it felt like a trip into her own past. The Philosophy Department, where Karl taught was next to the Neckar River in an ancient building called Alte Burse that had views of the river. She arrived just as a seminar ended and the students dispersed into the afternoon, discussing their plans for the evening on their way down the stairs. She saw Karl in the front of the classroom packing up papers. He looked up.

"Vega! Good timing! I'll just drop these papers off in my office. You might want to poke around for a few minutes. These are your old stomping grounds after all."

"Yes, it's nice to be back," she answered. "I'll wait outside on the steps."

"What a gorgeous day," said Karl as he joined her a few minutes later, "I hadn't really noticed until now. Would you like to take a walk on Neckar Island?" he asked casually. A long and narrow strip of land, Neckar Island, ran along the center of the river, easily accessible from a bridge at its beginning and end.

"I'd love to take a walk," agreed Vega. "I have your sister's belongings in my car at the parking lot. It's not very much," she added.

"I'll drive you there later and pick it up. I have a parking space here at the Institute. One of the few perks of my job!"

"You work in a beautiful place!"

"I am not complaining!"

"Did you grow up here?"

"Sarah and I grew up in Stuttgart," Karl answered, referring to the city about 30 km northeast of Tübingen. "But my parents were originally from Breslau. They were refugees after the war, when the Russians took over that part of Germany. They struggled, having to rebuild their entire existence, and we lived in very simple circumstances in an industrial suburb of the city. The apartment building we grew up in was very small. We did not have our own rooms. That's why Sarah and I were so close. We were forced to be. My parents never quite assimilated; most of their friends were other refugees from Schlesien." They had reached Neckar Bridge and now descended the steps down onto the tree shaded pedestrian path populated by students and people walking their dogs.

"You have come a long way!" said Vega.

Karl made a depreciating noise. "So they say!"

"You two were the only children?"

"Yes, Sarah and I only had each other. But I am five years younger than my sister, and therefore, even though we were close, I felt that I didn't really know her that well. She already had a life of her own by the time I came along."

"Was Sarah very close to her father?" Vega asked, feeling a little awkward, as if she did not really have the right to ask, but the photo of the little Sarah looking up to her father still stuck in her mind. It did not seem to bother Karl, because he answered without hesitation.

"I think Sarah and our father were very close when she was little, but he was gone when we were still quite young."

"Gone?" Vega prompted.

"He died in prison when I was twelve years old. By that time he had already spent three years behind bars."

"I am very sorry, Karl." Vega felt she was prodding an old wound, but at the same time Karl seemed ready to talk about his family.

"It was hard. Especially for my mother. She had to raise us without help from anybody. Without help from family, without the church, without government support. That's when Sarah changed. She became withdrawn, wouldn't talk to anybody. She became very thin and probably started taking drugs. It changed all of us. Nobody wanted to have anything to do with us after what my father had done. We were like outcasts."

"What had he done?" Vega dared ask, again feeling like an intruder on the slippery surface of her companion's soul.

Karl looked at her sharply. "He tried to kill a priest," he said curtly, then turned around abruptly, heading back toward the stairs. Vega had gone too far. He had revealed more than he had intended and he regretted it now. Vega understood his discomfort and they retraced their steps in silence. Alongside the island little rowboats floated lazily in the river, and young couples called out to each other with jokes and laughter. The afternoon was still warm and even though the shadows grew longer, the water of the placid Neckar still glittered in the May sunshine.

"Here is my car. I'll give you a lift to the parking lot."
Vega thanked him and got into the Volkswagen Passat. They reached her blue Polo without speaking, and Vega loaded Sarah's suitcase and box into Karl's trunk.

"Did Sarah travel to Asia?" she asked casually thinking of the mysterious scroll.

"Why do you want to know all this? What is your business with my sister?" asked Karl aggressively, standing next to his car, his arms crossed in front of his chest, suddenly suspicious and defensive.

"Look, I know this may seem like idle curiosity. I may have overstepped my boundaries, and if I did, I apologize. I don't want to violate your privacy Karl, but for some reason I came to care about Sarah. I want to understand what happened to her. How she ended up behind the Spring of Tears. I found her; she is now somehow part of my life too. I feel a certain responsibility. Maybe I shouldn't. But for some reason I feel her life should not disappear without any trace, with only those few pitiful remnants left." She pointed toward the box on Karl's backseat. Karl's posture relaxed a little, his arms at his sides.

"It's okay. I am a little on edge myself. I can't get over the image of Sarah lying on the metal slab in the morgue, white as a ghost. I ask myself the same question over and over again: Is this all her life amounts to? Is this all that's left, a body in a morgue under neon lights? All her talent, her beauty, her promise, her potential, it all ends here?" He looked at her with disbelief. Vega shook her head.

"I have been reading her letters again," he continued. "She did write to me, not very regularly, but she always let me know where she was. I made copies of the letters for your inspector. I don't know if it will do any good, but I want to do my part in trying to solve her murder. There must be a reason; there must be some sort of explanation. A life cannot end so senselessly," he muttered and pulled out a large manila envelope, which he handed to her.

"Is philosophy any help?" asked Vega meekly.

"No," Karl said. He got into his car and drove away.

Vega watched him disappear into the rush hour traffic then looked down at the envelope in her hands. Sarah's letters! She could not deny a rush of excitement at the thought of reading them and hearing Sarah's voice through them. But what was she thinking? She could not just read confidential material handed to her by a relative of a murder victim. But Karl had given her the envelope freely. As she turned it around she noticed it was not even sealed, just closed with a small removable metal clasp. Nobody would know if she read them. Quite possibly, these letters might help her unravel the mystery of Sarah's death. Already, Vega had turned on her heel and headed across the street into the majestic university library reading room. Inside she sat down next to a blond student with a ponytail at a dark wooden table and began to read.

New York, July 14,

Dear Karl,

Things are going well for me here in New York. I don't know why I am still feeling such despair. Found a little apartment. Actually it is just a room with a shower and a kitchenette (a hotplate and sink to be precise). I have to share the bathroom. But it is in a very charming brownstone building in Brooklyn and it has a window pointing toward Manhattan. If I stand at a particular spot and look out at the correct angle, I can see the Empire State Building. Today it is illuminated in patriotic red, white and blue. Did you know it changes colors according to holidays and occasions? It's green on St. Patrick's Day and pink on Valentines Day, and red and green for Christmas. You get the idea. I guess we are still close enough to Independence Day to justify the patriotic combo.

Spring of Tears

My neighbors here in the building are: A German engineering intern, a rather plumb, female disc jockey from Iowa, a Canadian film student, and across the street, lives a male, black photo model. Everybody seems quite nice. They have given me a reading lamp and two old saw horses, which combined with a defunct door made the desk I am sitting at. I am writing in the light of the little lamp, because it is very late, but nevertheless unbelievably hot. The sweat is dripping down my temples. I have the window wide open, but the air is so still you could cut it with a knife.

There is no way I could sleep in this heat. I am not the only one. People stay up all night here, I can hear them outside on the street, talking and laughing. A boom box is playing rap music very loudly. They wait until it gets a little cooler, around 3 or 4 in the morning. It's fine with me. It's hard for me to get through the night anyway. At least I am not awake by myself. New York suits me. It gives people the chance to start over, be who they want to be. Nobody here talks about where they came from. Somehow we are all people without a past. We forget the past, relish the present and anticipate a great future. I don't know about that last part, but I am sure I'll find some sort of work here. Right now I am just happy to deal with one day and one night at a time. Oh, they just switched off the light on the Empire State Building. It must be really late. I think I am going to sit on the stoop of my building for a bit. Maybe it's cooler there! More soon!

Love, your carefully hopeful sister,

Sarah

"Sarah knew she was damaged." Vega looked up. The library reading room was getting emptier, and the light outside of the neoclassical windows was fading. She still had a three-hour drive back home in front of her. Her family was probably beginning to get worried, but she could not stop reading now. Under the watchful eyes of the librarian on night duty she continued:

New York, August 14,

Dear Karl,

I found a job. It is not exactly a modeling job, but I am working with a photographer. He has a studio in Park Slope, close to Prospect Park here in Brooklyn. I help with developing and lighting. He is helping me with my portfolio so I can find an agent. His name is Gary. He is from Long Island, but he does not want to be reminded of that fact. He says very little and is always dressed in black (of course everybody is always dressed in black here). My neighbor, the male model helped me make the contact.

I feel comfortable with Gary in a very detached kind of way. We rarely talk, which suits me. He is not intrusive at all. He respects my privacy. If he only knew that my privacy consists of a huge hole of emptiness, right in the middle of myself, where the heart should be. But then again, how can I hurt so much, if I am all empty inside? Anyway, I am glad to be here, because I am always surrounded by people and noises, and even though I don't much talk to the people, I don't feel quite so alone. All the activity here in New York, with its never-ending lights, action, smells and movements fills up a little bit of the emptiness. I hope your Nietzsche class is going well and that you have some bright students, who can

appreciate what Friedrich and you have to say! Nietzsche

deserves the best. I still remember what you taught me about

him:

"Ich liebe die Untergehenden, denn sie sind die

Hinübergehenden und Pfeile der Sehnsucht zum anderen

Ufer." (I love those who are sinking, because they are the ones

in transition and arrows of longing to the other shore!)

Thinking about that, sometimes makes me feel better. But

probably all the arrows of longing I sent off must have fallen

into the water and never reached the other shore!

Love always from your fairly busy sister,

Sarah

It sounded to Vega as if Sarah had found a tentative home, with a few friends, a job, and even some furniture of her own. But she still did not seem to have much hope that it could last.

New York, September 7

Dear Karl,

I am afraid I'll have to leave here soon. Strange things are

happening. At first, I thought it's maybe all just a

coincidence, but now I can't believe that anymore. Two weeks

ago I came home from work and found my door unlocked. I

didn't think much of it, because Thomas has a key and so

does Rita, and they sometimes come in and borrow a chair or

a cup if they have visitors. When I walked into the room, the

little desk lamp was on like a spotlight. Maybe they left me a

note, I thought, and walked over to the desk. But instead of a note the lamp shone on a piece of paper with nothing but a big black cross on it right in the middle of my desk! I have to tell you it freaked me out! I ran upstairs and showed it to the others, but no one had seen the paper or any stranger in the house that day! They all tried to calm me down, but I could not find a rational explanation of how the cross got onto my desk. Still I decided to let the matter go. Then a week later I came home and again my door was ajar. This time I already had a bad feeling, and when I entered I saw that someone had pulled out all my clothes and scattered them around the room! I don't have much but it still was a mess! In the middle of the room my new white bathrobe was spread out, with a huge red stain right in the middle! The red liquid dripped down and formed a puddle on the floor! It looked like blood! I screamed and Thomas and Rita rushed in. They had to hold me, I was shaking so hard. The red liquid turned out to be wine, but the robe is ruined. I felt so vulnerable and violated. Someone broke into my room and did this to me. Of course it would not be hard to get in: there is the fire escape and then there are always people going in and out of the front door, it would be relatively easy to get access. I could not sleep alone in my room after this incident. Rita dragged her mattress down and stayed with me. She brought some of her New Age calming music and we listened to that and talked quietly in the dark. I don't want to leave, because I like my housemates here. But what should I do? Am I going crazy, Karl?

Your scared sister,

Sarah

Sarah's pessimism had apparently been justified. Her new home was no safe haven and she was scared of a real or imagined enemy, but in light of her death, the warning signs mentioned in the letter became more significant. Mesmerized, Vega read on.

New York, October 4,

Dear Karl,

I had to move out of Brooklyn. Another incident happened and that was the final straw for me. As you can imagine, after the cross and the wine, I was jittery and nervous each time I came home. But then a couple of weeks ago I woke up one morning and almost had a heart attack: next to my mattress on the floor lay a dead rat, it's head cut off from the rest of the body, it's blood all splattered around it! I was so terrified, I could not even scream! Someone had been in my room while I was sleeping and done this! I did not say anything to anyone, just went to the bathroom and threw up! Then I packed a bag and left. I checked into a small hotel in Manhattan under a different name.

Karl, that rat could have been me! I just quietly made a few runs to Brooklyn until I had all my clothes. Everything else I left behind. I'll never see Rita and Thomas again! But it's better this way. At the hotel nobody knows my name; it's pretty anonymous and cheap. I think I will be safe. Don't write to me anymore to the Brooklyn address. Write to my post office box! I also quit my job with Gary, because I think I can get some photo shoots now. Plus, I want to leave no trace.

I feel safer since I live in Manhattan and I don't have to take the subway all the time. The subway in New York reminds me of Dante's circles of hell. In the summer it stinks of urine and sweat, in the winter of wet wool, and in between it is flooded by filthy water, which brings out the rats that run over my feet. I don't need to see rats right now! The noise down in the shafts is truly infernal. It's a whole underground world down there and some of its inhabitants never leave it. They sleep on cardboard boxes in the stations, they beg and eat and shit down there. They don't need to leave. Even entertainment is provided. Yesterday I heard an Italian tenor sing an aria from Puccini's Tosca, and graffiti artists provide visual decoration on the white station tiles.

But for me it was easy to feel trapped down there, especially when I had to squeeze into a full train at rush hour and then went underneath the East River from Brooklyn to Manhattan. You can't breathe and when I imagined all that water above me, it really freaked me out! Since I live in Manhattan I can walk almost everywhere I need to go. I try to blend in, which is not very difficult, because everybody looks kind of eccentric and minds his or her own business.

Don't worry about me, I am okay! You have to concentrate on your own life! I am very happy that you met a girl you really like! And a Nietzsche student at that! How perfect. I am sure you two have brilliant and stimulating conversations, quoting Nietzsche to each other.

Love, your undercover sister,

Sarah

Vega's heart beat loudly against her ribcage. *"Karl, that rat could have been me!"* Sarah's words rang in her head. Why hadn't Karl done anything? A death threat, obviously directed against Sarah. He'd been busy, of course, with his career and his new girlfriend, plus Sarah told him not to worry. What could he have done anyway? Was this a direct connection to her murderer? Had the killer pursued Sarah all the way from New York to Strasbourg? Vega was interrupted by the gong announcing the closing of the library. At least she had missed rush hour. She packed up the papers and went over to the copy machine, where she made a set of photocopies of Sarah's letters. As she walked past the Ionian columns and down the gray marble steps of the grand library, the stillness and darkness of the night surrounded her like a tight coat. It felt a little too tight even.

Wednesday, May 20, Tübingen, 2:30 AM:

As night descended over the small university town of Tübingen, small groups of students migrated from one small bar or *Kneipe* to the other for a beer or two until closing time, but the majority of the old, medieval houses turned out their lights early. The Schlossberg, the castle mountain, lay in dark shadow, as a black silhouette in front of the moonlit sky and the sparking Neckar River below. Only one light stayed on past midnight in a window halfway up the hill. The window belonged to an apartment on the third floor of an old house with desirable views of the river and the Schönbuch Forest beyond. Inside the apartment, a man sat at a desk, his face buried in his hands. Scattered on the desk were books and manuscripts. A well-used copy of Nietzsche's *Thus Spoke Zarathustra* lay within easy reach, next to volumes by Kant, Hegel, Derrida, and Marcuse. Pages with handwritten script covered the rest of the desk's available surface. The handwriting looked erratic, irregular as if scrawled speedily, the letters leaning to the left, as they often do for left-handed writers. Some of the pages were torn out of notebooks or legal pads. Many had coffee stains on them, or discolorations of a less recognizable origin. The man fingered the pages and then took a sip from a glass containing a honey-colored liquid. He stared at a page with an illustration of a crudely drawn, black cross, with four equal arms, which thickened at the end into an elongated triangle shape.

A woman in a pink bathrobe entered the room. Her red hair looked tousled and her eyes squinted into the light, as if she had just woken up from a deep sleep. She walked over to the man and put her hand on his shoulder.

"Karl, it is two thirty in the morning. Aren't you coming to bed?"

The man looked up at her with red, bloodshot eyes.

"I should not have given copies of her letters to this woman. I know, she'll read them. She is a nosy busybody!"

The woman answered with exaggerated patience, as if she had rehearsed the words and said them before:

"You did not give the letters to the woman. She was just the messenger. They will go to the inspector investigating the case. He needs to see them; they may contain clues about what happened to Sarah. You did the right thing!"

"The inspector doesn't even understand German!" retorted Karl desperately.

"They have good translators. It's not like the Alsace is a third world country. It's just across the border. You had to do it, Karl; it was your duty."

"I should have done something a lot earlier, Leah," Karl burst out, "when I received these letters, when my sister was still alive!" Karl buried his face in his hands. "She was afraid; she felt she was in mortal danger. She tried to hide, because she knew someone was after her! And she told me so in her letters, repeatedly and in no uncertain terms. And what did I do? Nothing, I basically ignored her!"

"Karl, there is no sense beating up on yourself! You always supported your sister! Remember how often you sent her money and then the ticket to get back to Europe?" Leah put her hand on Karl's shoulder and felt his tense muscles underneath the thin fabric of his shirt.

"But I let her down when it counted most." Karl was not to be consoled.

"Karl, you couldn't know it was serious! Plus she made it out of New York safely, thanks to your financial support."

"Leah, I didn't read between the lines. I was so wrapped up in our engagement and the wedding preparations, I failed to get the message."

"Oh, so now it's my fault! Because you were involved with me and our relationship, you didn't pay enough attention to your precious sister, and that eventually cost her life. She was your older sister, for crying out loud, how come you were always responsible for her? How come you were not allowed to have a life of your own? How come I am to blame for selfishly asking for some time and attention too?"

"Leah, please calm down. Nobody is blaming you. It is all my fault entirely. I failed her and I'll have to live with that for the rest of my life."

"I'll have to live with that too, Karl, your endlessly guilty conscience! Why does she always have precedent over me and Rachel, even now that she is dead? We always had to cater to her needs. Whenever she honored us with her visits, as inconvenient as they were, we had to be at her beck and call!"

"Leah, she's dead! How can you be jealous of a dead woman?"

"Well, I for one won't miss her, and I am glad she is not around Rachel anymore. I did not like her around our daughter; she was so fixated on her; I did not know what she was up to, and I certainly did not like her influence! What a role model, a junkie and a vagabond!"

"You are being cruel and unfair now. Sarah loved Rachel more than anything on this world. More than she loved me. And she did not have much in this world." He pointed toward the box and the suitcase with Sarah's belongings.

"Are these her things?" asked Leah, a little shrill. "I don't want them in my house!"

"Leah, it's my house too and these things are precious to me." He took out the photograph of the young Sarah and her father, as well as the picture of Rachel and himself and put them on his desk. Leah's gaze softened a bit as she saw the photo of her daughter.

"How are we going to explain all this to Rachel?" she asked more calmly.

"We'll explain it to her when the time is right. And then I want to give her something that belonged to her aunt. I know Sarah would like that."

"What's there to give?" asked Leah contemptuously. "A few old books, an ashtray, and a scroll?" Karl pulled out the scroll and unrolled it. The huge red, monster with its crown of five skulls, holding the giant wheel divided into the six compartments appeared in the dim light of Karl's desk lamp.

"This is ghastly!" gasped Leah.

"Apparently it was precious to Sarah. She took it with her wherever she went. And she traveled light. She must have gotten it in India or Nepal."

"Don't remind me of that disaster!"

"Yes, I remember that you accused her of going there for the drugs in no uncertain words. I think she went there to get away from the drugs and from whoever was haunting her."

"You always made excuses for her, Karl. In your eyes she could do no wrong. You always saw her in a golden glow, when she seemed to stumble from one failure and disaster to the next in the eyes of the rest of us."

"Leah, whatever haunted or hunted my sister, I would not wish on anybody. She had to live with demons that you and I can barely imagine. She dealt with them as best as she could, until they caught up with her."

"I don't want to release those demons onto my daughter! It'll give her nightmares or worse!"

"I'll save this scroll for Rachel until she is old enough to make her own judgment."

"Hopefully that won't be for a long time, Karl. I am going to bed, good night," concluded the woman and pulled her bathrobe tighter around her crunched up, bony shoulders.

85

"Leah," said the man in a soft voice, as she was about to leave the room, "I am going to New York."

"You are what?" the woman spun around, incredulous.

"I am going to find Sarah's friend Gary and talk to him. I have to do this, for me and for Sarah."

"What about me and Rachel? Don't we count for anything? Don't we need you too?"

"You and Rachel are the most precious people in my life, you know that, but no, I don't think you need me as much as Sarah did and still does."

"Maybe soon we won't need you anymore at all!" she hurled the words at him, then left the room, sobbing with anger and frustration. The man sat alone at his desk again, staring at the pictures of his daughter and his sister.

Wednesday, May 20, 10 AM, Klingenthal:

Vega had missed a deadline for the first time in her career as a freelance writer. She sat at her kitchen counter, tired from a long night of reading and driving. In front of her sat the telephone and she waited for it to ring or for her fingers to be able to pick up the receiver and dial the number of the *Alsatian Monthly* editor's desk. Her stomach felt like a knot, and as she looked at the leftover pieces of bread and half-finished cereal bowls on the table in her not-so-tidy kitchen, she thought, "I guess, I am just a housewife after all, and not even a very good one at that". She had imagined her life in Europe a little differently: she had dreamt of living in France in a beautiful environment, great food, liberal politics, and with plenty of time to write. Before she had been so busy with her job and the kids that she always put off the novel she wanted to write. But here in the Alsace, she had imagined, she would have the inspiration and time to finally get the novel done. Instead she could not even complete a little assignment on a local attraction on deadline! What kind of a writer did that make her?

The telephone rang.

"You will never write for this magazine again!" the editor yelled into the receiver.

"I know, and I understand your frustration, Monsieur Harp," Vega answered guiltily.

"It's not like you are reporting from a war zone or anything. All you had to do was write about a local woman who has been dead for about thirteen hundred years!" M. Harp continued contemptuously.

"I know and I assure you that I had every intention to complete and submit my assignment, but an unfortunate and extraordinary event interfered!" she tried to explain and the sentence hung there for a few seconds in the telephone line.

"What extraordinary event?" barked Harp, who possessed, like many men in his field, an unusual amount of curiosity.

"I got involved in the investigation into the death of a local woman, who died very recently on Mont Ste Odile under suspicious circumstances," Vega answered, somewhat cryptically.

"Murder?" snapped M. Harp immediately, like a hound on a trail. "You are not by chance talking about the murdered German girl, are you?"

"I found her, or to be precise, I found her shoe, which led to the discovery of the body behind the Spring of Tears."

"Up on Mont Ste Odile?"

"Yes, while I was researching your story."

"How extraordinary," Harp concluded, now without a trace of anger in his voice. "I read about the case in the *Strasbourg Daily*, of course. We don't get a lot of murders in these parts."

"No, I don't expect you do," agreed Vega.

"Well, if you find out anything, let us know, will you?" he concluded.

"I certainly will, monsieur!" Vega replaced the receiver with a smile. That went much better than she had expected. At that moment she decided to write about Sarah. Not for the *Alsatian Monthly*, but for herself, and for Sarah, to give her life a closure, for Karl, and, a few years down the road, for Rachel, so she would remember the aunt who had loved her so much.

As Vega contemplated this life-changing decision, little bare feet patted into the kitchen. Stevie had caught a cold, playing with Mona in the mud, and had to stay home from school. He stood before Vega in his pajamas, blanket in hand and without any shoes. Vega picked him up.

"Stevie, the floors are cold and you are already sick. Where are your house shoes? Come back to bed." She carried him upstairs.

"Mom, can I ask you a question?"

"Of course you can, and even if I said no, you still would," said Vega.

"Don't say confusing words, Mom. You know who these two plastic figures are?" Vega looked at the two small action figures Stevie clutched in his left hand, the hand not holding his soft blanket, as she placed him down onto his bed and spread the blue covers with the stars and the moons over him.

"Are these Star Wars figures?" she asked, feeling pretty clueless about his army of small creatures.

"No, Mom, of course not. They are Dorgans. They are bad guys. See, they are red and black. Those are evil colors."

"Why are they evil colors?"

"Because they are dark like the night and red like blood."

"But strawberries are also red, and we love those, don't we? Especially with whipped cream. So red cannot be that bad."

"Green is also an evil color," insisted Stevie, undeterred.

"Green, like the grass and the trees? Why on earth would that be an evil color?"

"Remember Vincent - he didn't like green and he used it to paint evil things. You told me that yourself."

Vega remembered looking together with her children at the van Gogh's painting *Night Café in Arles* at the van Gogh retrospective in Paris last year. The boys were fascinated by the painting and discussed it in great detail: why the room looked so scary and gloomy, like a passageway leading to hell.

"I am glad you remember that, Stevie. Vincent used a special kind of green as a scary and strange color in some of his paintings, but that doesn't make green evil for all of us."

"I think it's evil."

"Then what are good colors in your opinion?"

"Yellow, Vincent painted all those yellow sunflowers and the sun."

Apparently the exhibition had made a great impression on her youngest son.

"Any other colors?"

"Gold."

"What about blue? Is blue good?'

"O no, blue is too dark. It is a primary color anyway."

"So are red and yellow, aren't they?"

"But yellow is the brightest color, and that makes it good."

"What about white? That's a bright color, isn't it?"

"Mom, white is not a color and you can't even see it anyway. I never use white in my pictures."

"But isn't white the opposite of black, and you told me that black is an evil color?"

"Mom, I don't want to argue anymore."

"We are not arguing, just chatting," said Vega and patted his little back.

"It's too hard to argue with parents," concluded Stevie.

"Does that mean we don't need any evil colors then?"

"Mom, you are getting away with it! I knew it; that's why I don't want to argue with you anymore!"

Stevie was unconvinced as he turned toward the wall and pulled his blanket tightly around himself, holding his two favorite stuffed animals in his arms. Vega sat at his bedside for a little longer, stroking his back, thinking how much she loved this stubborn, smart, funny little being and how much she wanted to keep him safe. After less than three minutes she heard the deep, regular breath, telling her he was asleep. She thought about Sarah and how lonely and empty her life must have been, except for her few visits to see Rachel and Karl. Sitting in the wicker chair in a spot of sunlight coming through the window in Stevie's room she continued reading.

November 7,

Dear Karl,

Yesterday I went on a modeling job. It was for sunglasses, even though it is winter here. But you know how they always shoot out of season, so they can be ready as soon as the first sunrays come back out. I was glad for the sunglasses, because I could cover up the dark bags under my eyes from not sleeping. I was supposed to be there at 9 AM, which is very early for me, so I got there at 10:30 AM and the crew was really angry. They said I was wasting their time and money! The only person not yelling at me was the photographer. He looked at me kindly and even asked, if I wanted to go to a concert with him that night. I said okay, because I didn't want to be rude and get him mad as well. After the shoot I walked down 7th Avenue and it was so cold that it sucked the breath right out of my lungs. The wind just hurtled down the Avenue, as if it were icy water building up speed in a narrow canyon. It almost knocked me over. I had to lean into the wind with all my strength. In some strange way it felt good, because it hurt so much, it made me feel alive, or at least I felt something at all. At night I went to the Ritz on East 4th street to a Joe Cocker concert with the photographer. It was loud, dark and crowded. Joe Cocker did his weird contortions on stage. People were dancing; neo punks with lots of black eye shadow and torn stockings. At least we didn't have to talk, because of the music and the noise. At two in the morning the club closed and my date walked me home. He must have been on speed or something, because suddenly he talked nonstop. He talked about what kind of music he likes and all I could think of was that I wanted him to be quiet. I was afraid he'd come upstairs with me, so I invented an infectious disease, which I did not want to pass on to him. I think we were both relieved when we could part in front of the hotel. I watched him walk down the Bowery and was glad to see him go. I bet you never feel this way with Leah. What's the secret?

Love, Your lonely sister,

Sarah

Poor Sarah! Relationships did not come easy for her. Maybe she had reason to be suspicious and distrustful. Vega read on.

New York, November 28,

Dear Karl,

Yesterday was Thanksgiving. I didn't know that Americans make such a big deal out this holiday, so I just hung out in my room and did not have any plans. Suddenly the receptionist called and said someone was there to see me. I could not imagine who it could be, but I went downstairs to the lobby (lobby is really an exaggeration, because it is just a little entrance space with green wall paint and neon lighting).

Gary was waiting there for me. He asked if I wanted to go and have some coffee, so I said yes, because I had nothing else to do and I hadn't had any breakfast yet. We went to the corner coffee shop and I asked him: "How did you find me?" He said he got my address from my agency. Then he asked, if I wanted to come back to work for him again. I told him that I was doing okay and that I didn't want to commute to Brooklyn every day. He nodded and then we just sat there and drank coffee and smoked cigarettes. After a while he said that he kind of missed me. I laughed and joked that I didn't think he would notice that I was gone. He asked if I wanted to go out with him, but I still didn't get it, so I said: "Where to?" He said: "How about to the movies?" That was okay with me, so we walked over to Bleeker Street cinema and saw a French matinee movie with subtitles. I felt like being in a Woody Allan movie, except that Gary hardly ever says anything and Woody Allen never shuts up. After the movie we went to a small deli and had turkey meat with gravy and cranberry sauce and mashed potatoes. A real Thanksgiving meal, as Gary told me. It was quite good! But after dinner I started feeling very antsy and fidgety. I couldn't stop coughing and my bones were aching! I told Gary, I had to go, and he wanted to know if we could meet again. I said sure. So you see little brother, I am working on my relationship skills. You can be a little bit proud of me, but not as proud as I am of you!

Your sister,

Sarah

"Sarah was trying hard to change her insular life style," Vega thought. "Maybe she was inspired by her brother. She wanted to give the relationship with Gary a chance."

New York, December 15

Dear Karl,

Congratulations on your engagement! Of course I want to come to your wedding in the spring! How could I not? My only brother getting married, I wouldn't miss it for the world! I am so proud of you and can't wait to meet Leah. If things continue to unravel for me in New York as they have been, I might even be back sooner! Unfortunately I had a run in with a photographer during a photo shoot. It wasn't pleasant and I don't think I'll get modeling work any time soon after this. Word travels fast in this business. They were doing a piece about "heroin chic", you know, I was supposed to look really strung out and skinny, which is not hard for me to do, because that's pretty much how I look right now anyway. So, I had to lie on a sofa in torn jeans and a sweater with holes and stare vacantly at the ceiling. Of course the sofa is for sale for a mere $5,900, the jeans can be purchased (holes and all) at a bargain price of $395 and the sweater is a unique piece available at Bloomingdale's for under $1,000, not to mention the diamond studded navel adornment in the shape of a safety pin for a trifling $13,500! My eyes were all made up with large black smudges under them and the skin all pale to make me look even more sickly. All that was not hard to do. But then, one of the camera assistants had the glorious idea to include some junkie paraphernalia in the picture, like a spoon *and a candle and a belt, casually lying on the table. That freaked me out! I blew a fuse. I started yelling that I wasn't going to support the exploitation and commercialization of junkies. I screamed at him: "It's not a glamorous habit to be glorified in a glossy magazine, and it ruins people's lives every day!" They all looked at me, as if I came from a different planet. "Listen Lady," said the main photographer finally, "we didn't ask for your opinion and a lecture on social issues." I said: "But it's my body, you are using!" They looked at each other with an annoyed expression, and then they said: "That's what we are paying you for. It's your job. If you don't like it, get out!" So they threw me out. I knew, it wasn't cool, but you know, sometimes I just can't control my temper, it always gets me into trouble. I walked down 5th Ave, still with that awful make-up on, in my own jeans, torn and tattered much more economically, and I felt like shit. The whole thing just hit a little too close to home. I have to find some other way to make money, but don't worry, little brother, I'll find something. At least I feel safe, no more incidents since I moved to Manhattan. Take care of yourself and your young bride to be!*

Love from your broke sister,

Sarah

"Every time things were looking up for Sarah, something happened that destroyed all her hopes," Vega mused. "It must have been so hard for her to keep going."

New York, December 26

Dear Karl,

Christmas time in New York can be very romantic, I guess, if you have a lot of money and wear warm fur coats and shop on 5th Avenue. Of course none of the above mentioned factors apply to me. As you know I am allergic to Christian holidays. Here in New York there are plenty of people like me. People without family and money and Christmas obligations, like buying presents or going to Christmas parties. By the way, I am sorry for not sending you anything and even this letter comes too late to count as a Christmas greeting. O well, I know you will forgive me, but will Leah? I know she was the one who bought the card with the gold background, and I know you were the one who put $100 inside the envelope! Thank you, I really did need that! Well, actually I went to one party, kind of. Gary invited me to go to visit his mother with him in Long Island. I really didn't want to go. I thought it was not a good idea and would probably turn into a disaster, and it did! I don't know why he hasn't given up on me yet, why he still comes around. I am such a wreck and don't deserve this kind of attention. I don't know why I gave in and went along. I guess it was just a combination of monotonous gray days, a clammy hotel room and cheap take - out food. I put some make-up on and the best frock I have left and then we took the Long Island Express out to Garden City. What an ugly train, with sticky floors and orange plastic seats! Gary tried to make the journey a little more pleasant by bringing a newly published photography book along, entitled "Shades of Gray: New York seen through the

Eyes of 20 Black and White Photographers". It was the Christmas present for his mother. One of the photographs in the book is his. It's a black and white shot of a tree in Central Park in winter without leaves seen from below. I thought it looked just like any of the hundreds of trees passing by in front of the train window, but I didn't say anything. It was Christmas Day after all and I didn't want to be rude. His mother picked us up at the train station in a white Chevy, a really big old car. She had permed and dyed red hair and wore a two-piece tweed suit with a matching handbag. The moment we set eyes on each other, we knew this wasn't going to work. She welcomed me with a stiff upper lip and ushered us into the car. Then she started talking non-stop. Now I know why Gary is so quiet, he never had a chance to practice his speech! When we entered the house it was stifling hot, all the windows were tightly shut and the rooms were cramped full of furniture and knick-knack. On the yellow couch in the living room with stiff, matching pillows sat a catholic priest waiting for us! I must have stared at him in total disbelief, I was in such shock. He looked just like our priest, when we were children, Father Emanuel. How can that be, I thought, how can he be here in this house, in America all the way across the ocean? Gary's mother made the introductions, a friend of the family, a coincidence, obviously, but I could not handle it. It was too much! I could not stay. I excused myself, not very well, I am afraid. Gary looked heartbroken, but his mother seemed rather relieved not having to spend her Christmas dinner with me. Gary insisted on driving me back to the train station. I apologized and tried

to come up with an explanation, I told him that I had had
very bad experiences with priests, that one ruined our lives,
and that he resembled his mother's friend too much for me to
be comfortable being around him. We spent over an hour
sitting in his mother's car in the parking lot of the Long
Island Railroad. It was a gray day and it was getting dark
early. Not a lot of trains were running on Christmas day and
we had to wait for a long time. So I told Gary about Father
Emanuel, what he had done to me. I owed him at least that
much. When I finally told Dad what went on, he went to
confront Emanuel and then you know the rest. Gary listened
very patiently and silently. He is a good listener, which he no
doubt learned being around his mom. I think he forgave me.
He is some kind of saint or something. But I messed up
again, ruined another Christmas. I could not help it.
Hopefully I did not spoil your Christmas mood. Enjoy your
holidays with Leah. Tübingen in the snow is so romantic!
Happy New Year, I look forward to seeing you in the spring!
Love from your messed-up sister,
Sarah

"That did not sound good." Vega looked up and heard a car drive up to the house. She was startled out of her reverie. The car would be the car pool delivering Daniel from school. It was spring and not winter, she reminded herself. She was in the Alsace, not New York and her children were safe. Vega ran downstairs, welcomed Daniel and waved to Monique, the mother of his friend Jacques, who had driven him home and was now taking off toward Hagenau. As she prepared a snack of apples and yogurt for Daniel and helped him get ready to do his homework, she thought about the young Sarah, who had been barely older than her son. If she read correctly between the lines, Father Emanuel could have tried to molest her. That would explain why she had such low self esteem, why she obviously was not interested in sex, and why Catholic priests freaked her out. It helped explain why Sarah had resorted to drugs, but not why she was murdered.

Thursday, May 21, 10 AM, Strasbourg:

Stevie was back in school, happy to be with his friends again. The day was warm and the air smelled like spring. Robins and blackbirds populated the still flowering peach trees lining the boulevards. They sang as loudly as possible, as if to remind the pedestrians below to look up and see them perched on pink flowered branches in front of an aquamarine blue sky. Vega decided to walk across the Place de la Cathedrale, which sparkled in the spring sunlight, to the Fine Arts Museum of Strasbourg. She had not been inside the museum for a long time and was surprised to see how much it had changed since. Large, green banners announced a special exhibit of Jean Arp, the quintessential Alsatian Dadaist artist. For some reason she always expected the museum to stay the same, a time capsule in a changing world. It was comforting to enter the hushed marble entrance rotunda with the quietly babbling fountain in the middle and the majestic staircase leading to the upper floor. Vega knew it had been here for centuries in the past and it would be here for centuries to come, still looking the same, still providing a place of respite and contemplation. Vega moved through the special exhibition galleries relatively quickly. She was looking for the Asian collection, or at least someone with knowledge about Asian Art.

When Vega reached the Asian Gallery, she found a well-groomed gray haired woman speaking to what looked like a group of third graders. They stood in front of a Japanese Buddha, who sat on an enormous gold-gilded lotus throne.

"Amida," the woman, who was apparently a museum docent, said, "is believed to be the Buddha of the Western Paradise, supposedly a very wonderful place, where you are reborn in a lotus pond, sitting on a lotus flower, if you die with Amida's name on your lips."

A girl with blond curls fidgeted and tried to get her girlfriend's attention, by tickling her on her upper arm. The brown eyes of two little boys started to wander toward the ceiling.

The docent noticed and walked over to the boys as she continued. "In this paradise hundreds of bluebirds sit in the trees and sing the name of *Buddha,* the *Dharma* and the *Sangha;* the Buddha, his teaching and the community. Diamonds as big as ostrich eggs reflect the light and create sparkling specks on the grass and the water."

The blond girl and her friend held hands now and swung them back and forth in rhythmical fashion, giggling quietly. The docent turned her back to the Buddha statue and faced the students squarely.

"Children, what do you think a paradise should look like?" she finally asked.

After a short pause, little hands shot in the air, and the docent called on the students, one after the other.

"I think there should be as many videogames as you want, and you could play them all day," a little boy said, and his friends nodded eagerly.

"I think there should be lots of little kittens and owls to play with and they should all be very tame and sweet," said the little blond girl, who had dropped her friends hand to answer.

"I think there should be real Pokémon that you can catch and play with," another little boy said.

"There would be no war and nobody could get sick," a pale little boy said.

"An excellent wish; a world of peace and health. Now you are getting the idea of Amida's Western Paradise. It can be what each person is secretly wishing for," the docent concluded. The classroom teacher thanked her and ushered her class back to the rotunda.

"I really liked your question. It regained the children's attention and it made them think," Vega complimented her.

"Thank you. It is not always easy to show them that there is a connection between these works of art and their own little lives."

"We all have fantasies of paradise," Vega admitted.

"Yes, mine right now is to sit down and take a break. I have been on my feet all morning," conceded the docent, who moved toward a bench in the middle of the gallery. "Is there anything I can help you with, any question I can answer for you?" she added kindly as she sat down. Vega joined her on the bench and pulled out the picture of Sarah's scroll.

"Can you tell me more about this?" Vega asked.

"It is a Tibetan *thangka*," the docent observed. "It is a kind of mandala. I think it's called a wheel of life, and these six sections are the realms of rebirth: hell, the heaven of the gods, the realm of humans, and the realm of animals. We have a few *thangkas* here in the Asian Gallery, but I don't remember all the details about them."

"What do you mean with realms of rebirth?" asked Vega.

"Well, Tibetan Buddhists believe that we are all caught in the Wheel of Birth and Rebirth, which the lord of death, Yama, clutches in his claws," she began.

"Yama would be the red monster behind the wheel with the skulls on his head?" Vega clarified.

"Precisely. Now, depending on our Karma, after death we are either reborn into a better or worse realm of existence. See, the realm of the gods is very nice, they have a charmed life; but it will not last. They will use up all their good Karma and then be born into the realm of humans or even the realm of animals or hell down here." She pointed to the realm of hell on the picture.

"Karma means the good or bad deeds we do, right?" Vega confirmed.

"Karma simply means action. It describes a system of cause and effect. Whatever you do has an effect on you and onto others. Let's say, if I were about to slap your face. Excuse the inappropriate example . . ." she began and Vega had to smile at the thought of this kind and gentle lady slapping her.

"Well, if I did, then we both would be linked by Karma from then on. It would become my Karma to make up for the injustice I did to you. It would become your Karma to help me make up for it, by forgiving me. You see how it links us? Now, if you complained about my action to this guard over there,"- she pointed to a uniformed museum guard who stood discreetly in a corner of the gallery - "and if he came over and threw me out of the museum because of my behavior or even called the police, because of your complaint, then our Karma would be further intertwined. Now, you owe me for ruining my career, here at the museum and the guard gets involved too, because he threw me out. This may affect his life and Karma in a negative way."

"Crime and punishment," Vega muttered.

"Not exactly. Karma is not permanent. It is just an effect that was caused by an action and it will be replaced by another consequence or disappear through a different action."

"It's a complicated system," Vega remarked.

"The artist who painted this *thangka* tried to make it as simple as possible," the docent continued. "See these monks in maroon robes? Due to their meditation and Buddhist practice they are ascending into higher realms of rebirth, such as the realm of humans, who have choices and therefore are the luckiest of them all."

"And these scary figures descending in the same circle, who are they?"

"Those are criminals, people making bad choices, hurting others; they will be reborn in the realms of the giants or ghosts or hell."

"There is a realm of ghosts?" Vega asked, thinking of Stevie and his insistence on the existence of ghosts.

"Yes, Tibetan Buddhists believe that not all sentient beings are visible to us."

"My son would probably agree with them."

"Most children would." The docent laughed.

"Just one more question, if you don't mind. What are these three animals in the center?"

"The rooster, the pig and the snake are the symbols for the three poisons which lie at the root of all suffering and Karma. They represent greed or jealousy, ignorance, and anger or hatred. If we can overcome them, then we can escape the wheel of life and the clutches of death."

"Anger, ignorance, and greed."

"Yes, Buddhists believe they are the real enemies of peace of mind and peace on earth."

"This is a lot to think about. Thank you, you were very helpful," Vega said and got up from the bench.

"That's what I am here for," said the docent, pleased. On her way to the rotunda, Vega paused in front of the Amida Buddha. He seemed to smile at her behind heavy eyelids, sitting on his lotus throne in supreme dignity and calmness, his hands in his lap, legs folded in the lotus position, soles facing upward. His head was covered with orderly, small locks, curling in clockwise direction, like his thoughts, controlled through discipline and meditation. How can a mere mortal ever achieve such mind control, Vega thought, as she noticed her own thoughts straying in the direction of lunch. Amida seemed completely relaxed and totally aware at the same time. Nothing would disturb his peace of mind. He must have overcome ignorance, anger, and greed, she thought. Sarah must have felt that she was entangled in the system of cause and effect, of ascending and descending Karma, and that it was creating the personal hell she lived in, far away from paradise. She looked back at the still smiling Amida Buddha.

"It must be nice to live in the Western Paradise," Vega murmured to him quietly. He smiled back serenely in the affirmative.

On the steps in front of the museum, Vega was greeted by the bright May sunshine, warm and soothing after the cool darkness of the museum. She decided to walk along the river and have lunch on the small island Petit France. As it was such a beautiful day, she continued along the l'Isle toward the center city and the Rue de l'Outre. The tobacco store had just reopened after its lunch break when she entered.

"Ah, madame, what brings you here today, it is not raining and I doubt you have started a smoking habit since I saw you last?" Jean greeted her.

"I have brought you a new *Crime and Punishment,* " she smiled and handed him a new paperback book.

"How kind of you. I did not expect to get that one back," Jean said, leafing through the pages. "Did you read it?" he asked looking up

"Years ago. I reread parts of it," said Vega. "I'm wondering what intrigued Sarah about the story. Did she feel guilt over something she did? Was she more than just the innocent victim?"

Jean leaned against the counter, making himself more comfortable. The small store was empty.

"Like Raskolnikov? Strange that you would ask that," he began. "I have been thinking along similar lines. Sarah was not an 'innocent' girl. She had been around. She might have been the trigger, unwillingly I am sure, for what happened to her. There is something I remembered since your last visit. There were a couple of men, who hung around the neighborhood. One was short and skinny, with a ponytail and a worn leather jacket. I figured it was her dealer, and I told the police about him, because none of the neighbors want the likes of him around here. But there was another one. He seemed to watch Sarah. I saw him through the store window, right across the square. He sat in the bistro a lot, reading the paper. He drove a blue BMW with German number plates."

A customer entered, an old man with a bushy white mustache and corduroy pants. Jean greeted him by name and fetched a specific brand of pipe tobacco, unprompted. The man paid, mumbled a greeting, and left the store.

"Where was I?" Jean began again. "I can't close the store and have a coffee because I just returned from lunch. I am sorry for the interruption."

"You were talking about a man with a blue BMW," Vega reminded him. "How do you know he had anything to do with Sarah?"

"Because she got into the car and drove away with him."

"When was that?" Vega snapped to attention.

"Shortly before she died," Jean continued.

"Does the police know about this?"

"No, I just remembered."

"You need to tell them. Do you remember what he looked like?"

"I only saw him from afar; he never came near the store. He was middle-aged, stoutly built, wore good suits, sunglasses."

"A drug dealer?"

"Could be. But why did he spend so much time here, watching Sarah's building? I only put two and two together after you told me about Sarah's death. Before that, none of this seemed significant, and it wasn't my business with whom Sarah got into a car."

"I understand. But he might be important. I think it would be a good idea to call the inspector right away." Vega gave him Bonacourt's card. Three customers entered the store. She waved to Jean and left.

Friday, May 22, New York City, 2 PM:

Karl sat in the taxicab in the middle of Brooklyn Bridge and watched the rain splattering onto the window shield, while the car sat absolutely still amidst the furious honking of the drivers around them. His driver joined into the chorus, which did nothing to advance their progress any further. Karl clutched the book *Shades of Gray*. The page with Gary's picture was marked with a yellow sticky. The publisher had given him Gary's contact information and he had an appointment with the photographer in fifteen minutes, if they were going to ever move again! Thirty-five minutes later, he stood in the sparse, gray entryway of Gary's studio on Park Slope in Brooklyn, apologizing for the delay.

Gary smiled. "Don't worry about it. I know that the way from Manhattan to Brooklyn is a lot longer, than the reverse. Want some coffee?"

Karl nodded. Instinctively he liked this young man in his gray turtleneck and black jeans. He seemed calm and unpretentious. Through Sarah's letters, he felt as if he knew him. They sat in Gary's cluttered but spacious studio, next to camera equipment, in front of a photo backdrop at a low glass table.

"This is where Sarah worked?" Karl asked looking around.

"Yes, she helped in the darkroom, over there, she also assisted at photo shoots, and she scheduled appointments and did some of my paperwork. Clients liked her. She was quiet, calm, and she was beautiful."

Karl tried to picture his sister in this environment, and succeeded. She would not have been out of place here.

"Gary, thank you for meeting me. You know why I am here?"

"Not really. My publicist told me you were Sarah's brother, and I told her that of course I would see you. How is Sarah?"

"She is dead, Gary."

Gary stood up impulsively and exclaimed: "But how in the world? What happened? An overdose?"

"I am sorry to break it to you like that, Gary, but she was killed. That's really why I am here."

"I'll be damned," said Gary, sitting down and shaking his head. "She was on a road to self-destruction, I have to admit, but murder, I never would have thought …"

"Gary, I need to know what happened in the end, her final weeks here in New York."

"I'll tell you all I know, but it really isn't that much."

"You were the closest she had to a friend here. She wrote in her letters about you, about Thanksgiving, Christmas," Karl insisted.

"Don't remind me of that disastrous Christmas visit," Gary replied pacing up and down his studio.

"It's the only reason I found you. She mentioned the book with your photograph: *Shades of Gray*." Karl held up his copy.

"I don't think she thought very much of my photographs," Gary began with a smile. "But, you are right," he continued, "I tried to be her friend, and maybe even more. I liked her, she was beautiful and she was mysterious. But in the end, I came to the conclusion that her elusive behavior and mysterious ways were really just the cover for a very damaged and empty soul."

Karl cringed hearing these words. They echoed too closely what he had heard from Leah, over and over again. "She wrote to me about death threats, when she still lived in her apartment in Brooklyn. What do you know about that?" he ventured.

"Yes, I know, she was afraid that someone followed her, was after her. She sometimes behaved like a character in a spy movie. Changing subways, buses, trying to loose a tail. I was never sure there was much to it. But now, her death changes everything." Gary looked at Karl. "I am sorry, I don't mean to sound callous about your sister. I cared for her very much, but I was disappointed and hurt by her as well. She never let me get close to her, she never really trusted me, until I finally decided that whatever was underneath the surface was beyond repair. She knew she was damaged and she did not want help. I felt there was nothing I could do for her. But maybe I was wrong…"

"Gary, I feel guilty too, as if I could or should have prevented her death. I received her letters, she described threats, someone in her bedroom, at night, cutting off the head of a rat and leaving it there for her to see, and I did nothing about it. I just ignored it, went on with my life. Now I feel that I missed something. I want to get to the bottom of this, if I can. That's why I am here."

"I understand. I also feel that maybe I should have done more. Let me try to remember: Christmas. You know she freaked out about my mother's guest, the Jesuit priest? She had a real fit about him. Afterward she told me how a priest resembling my mother's friend once ruined her and your lives?"

Karl took a deep breath. "When Sarah was fourteen and I was nine, my father attacked our local parish priest, who was a Jesuit priest, and according to Sarah's letter he happened to look like your mother's guest. My father attacked him and paralyzed one side of the priest's body. He has been in a wheelchair ever since. My father was sentenced to twenty-five years in prison, but he died after only three. My mother had to raise us without any financial or moral support from anybody. We were outcasts. Sarah always blamed the Jesuit for our misfortune; she was fiercely loyal to our dad. I never quite understood why he did it. He was an atheist; my mother was very devout, but she became very bitter after the incident. She used to make us go to church, but after what happened, we were not welcome there anymore." Karl stopped. "How could that have anything to do with Sarah's death?"

"I don't know," acknowledged Gary. "She felt very threatened by the Catholic church. One of the treats she received was a black cross, and once, I remember we had to duck into a movie theater in the middle of the afternoon, because she saw a Jesuit priest following her in lower Manhattan."

"Gary, you can't suggest in earnest that a priest murdered my sister? What would be the motivation?"

"I am not suggesting anything. I am just trying to think about details of the time I spent with Sarah. That priest did terrible damage to Sarah."

"Our parish priest, Father Emanuel, the one my father attacked? You think he molested her?"

"At least he tried. Your sister told me on that Christmas day in the car what happened. Father Emanuel had tried to touch her when she was thirteen. He told Sarah her that she had reached the age when lust swells up between a woman's legs or something like that, and that she had to practice to resist that evil feeling. He was going to show her how to do it. She was supposed to pray and resist feeling anything, while he touched her. At first she almost believed him, but then he wanted to 'practice' every week. So she told your dad."

"Oh my God, I had no idea. That's what drove my dad to confront the priest and set the events in motion."

"She blamed herself for what happened to your father. She punished herself. She didn't want to forget."

"But she did not kill herself! Someone else did," insisted Karl.

"That is true and I have no explanation for that. You came all the way to New York to find the missing pieces. It seems to me the missing pieces to the whole picture are still back at home and in your past."

"Maybe you are right. I've never pursued digging into the incident with Father Emanuel and my mother never encouraged us to talk about it. She blamed my father for all our troubles."

"Could Sarah's death be drug related?" Gary asked cautiously.

Karl grimaced. "She had a considerable amount of heroin in her blood at the time of death, but not enough to kill her."

Karl neglected to mention that the killer had blinded Sarah. He could not bring himself to speak about this detail and felt he didn't want to reveal this final indignity to Sarah's former friend. Both men thought about drug dealers and what they were capable of, but did not vocalize their thoughts.

"She lived on the edge," Gary concluded, "but I did not know she lived so close to the abyss."

He got up and Karl followed. Apparently the meeting was over. Karl felt that Gary hadn't held back, that he was as forthcoming as possible, but still he wanted to know more, wanted this trip to New York yield more results than a vague suggestion to dig up their old childhood priest.

"Is there anything more you can tell me, anything at all?" Karl almost pleaded with the young photographer.

Gary hesitated. "Well, toward the end of her stay she came here one night, it must have been two or three in the morning. She knocked at my window and when I opened she said: 'I can't go home. He is waiting for me. He found me. He'll never let me be, he's still after me'. She was really frantic, so I let her in and asked: 'Who found you?' 'The Nazi,' she said. I told her, there where no more Nazis, but she insisted and said: 'That's what you think, but the Nazis are still alive and well'. 'What does he want from you? What do you have to do with him?' I asked. She said, 'I know what he wants, but he's not going to get it. Not after all I've been through.' 'What does he want?' I asked again. 'He wants the proof of his crimes. That's what my father discovered. My father died for it, that's how important it is. I know as long as I have it, he won't be at peace, and I am not going to give it to him,' she said with a crazy laugh. 'I am not going to let him have his peace.' 'But look at you,' I said, 'you are a wreck yourself! You are ruining yourself for this proof, whatever it is!' She said: 'I wish I knew what it is. It's in the picture, but dad did not have enough time to explain it.' She was shivering and talking gibberish. I finally said, 'Okay, you can sleep on the couch'. I couldn't deal with her anymore; I had a job early the next morning. So I gave her a blanket and went back to bed. I don't know, if it means anything, but unfortunately that's all I know. Sorry, Karl. I really hope you find whoever did this to your sister. She was messed up, but she did not deserve to die like this."

Karl nodded, thanked his host, and walked out into the still pouring rain of a gray Brooklyn twilight. He took the subway back to his hotel in Manhattan and smelled the wet wool Sarah had written about; he even saw a rat running across the platform. He thought about her description of Dante's inferno, and gave a dollar to a musician playing Vivaldi on the violin in the middle of the transfer tunnel. Karl tried to picture Sarah here and succeeded. Why had he never come to visit her in New York while she was still alive? Was it possible that someone had followed and found her here? What was this talk about Nazis? Both he and Sarah were born many years after the end of WWII and the collapse of the Nazi regime. How could Nazis play any role in their lives?

By the time Karl emerged from the subway tunnels it was dark. The rain had stopped and he walked slowly through the wet streets to his small hotel in lower Manhattan. The small streets south of Soho were eerily empty until suddenly two shadows peeled themselves away from the glistening walls and jumped at him. Before he knew it, he felt the cold blade of a knife tip touching his throat.

"Empty your pockets," demanded a muffled voice.

Karl obeyed shakily, handing over his wallet with credit cards and five hundred dollars in traveler checks. His assailant's partner took the bounty and gave out a low and pleased laugh.

"What else you have?"

Karl felt hands patting him down feeling under his raincoat, along his shoulders, his back, his legs. He did not dare to move. They found his camera and took it. Satisfied that they had extracted all his valuables, they hit him over the head with a baseball bat and disappeared into the night.

When Karl regained consciousness a couple of hours later, bleeding and wet, he managed to crawl to his hotel, which was only a block away. The receptionist eyed him suspiciously, but finally agreed to get him some ice for the wound and to call the police. By the time they came, he sat on his bed in the hotel room, in dry clothes but still throbbing with pain. They were not optimistic about the chances of either catching the muggers or retrieving his possessions. They told him to call his credit card company immediately, but probably it was already too late. He thanked them for the advice and they left. How easy it was to get hurt in this city, he thought. And yet, Sarah had survived New York and found death in the peaceful Rhine Valley. He wondered whether to call Leah. He knew she would be beside herself, upset and probably hysterical, blaming him for embarking on such a fool's errand in New York. So he decided to wait until he felt better. Luckily he had already bought the gift for his daughter Rachel. It lay right next to him on the bed: a big ladybug stuffed animal from FAO Schwartz.

Friday, May 22, 12:30 PM, Obernai:

The lunch crowd at the *Golden Swan* was noisy and impatient. They had had their beer or their apple cider and now they wanted fresh venison! Mme. Merrier had small sweat beads on her upper lips and at the temples. She carried three empty beer steins in each hand and maneuvered skillfully though the crowd to the counter. Amidst the chaos, calm as the eye of the storm, sat M. Bonacourt at his usual table. No impatience radiated from his composed face, only supreme concentration and attention to the words Vega, sitting opposite of him, was saying. Mme. Merrier glanced over to them regretfully. There was no way she could sit down casually with them and learn about the latest findings in the investigation. She snatched three plates loaded with Spätzle and venison topped with wild mushrooms in red wine sauce and delivered them to the nearest table. Appreciative cheers from the guests welcomed her. Mme. Merrier, a victim of her own success, was prevented from listening in on the conversation between Vega and M. Bonacourt. She put M. Bonacourt out of her mind and served more pungent smelling plates. Soon a content hum settled over the *Gaststube*. A gray cat with one white paw snuck in smoothly from the hallway in the hope of a scrap of meat. Waiting for the right moment Wilbur the cat watched from behind the flourishing geraniums and petunias in flowerpots outside of the *Gaststube* windows.

"So he hasn't called you and told you about the man with the blue BMW?" Vega asked incredulously, as she topped her meal with a generous sip of Alsatian wine. "I gave him your card and stressed that this information could be crucial!" She shook her head in disbelief.

"Not a word. We know about the other man, the alleged dealer, everybody gave a description of him, including Mme. Gluck and the tenants. We think we can track him down through Sarah's telephone records. But there is no record of the man with the BMW, all the telephone calls Sarah received or made, were either with her brother, her dealer, or the travel agency she worked for. But I think I have an explanation for M. Bonnard's silence. We checked the record of the neighborhood tobacconist after we visited him following Sarah Parker's death. He is on record for a felony. Hit and run, accidental manslaughter."

"He killed a person?" Vega could not believe her ears.

"Not intentionally, but yes, a young woman died because she was hit by Monsieur Bonnard's car. He does not have a driver's license and will not possess one for a long time."

"So he has just turned from a witness into a suspect?" Vega asked.

"No one can be excluded yet," M. Bonacourt stated professionally.

"Not even her brother?"

"Well, theoretically not. But speaking about Karl Parker: He has e-mailed me from New York, where he spoke to the victim's former employer."

"Gary," thought Vega. Karl finally felt the urgency and flew to New York to meet with Sarah's former employer, who was of course more, but she could obviously not admit to knowing that.

"Did he find out anything?" she asked innocently.

"Sarah told her former employer Gary that Nazis were pursuing her and mentioned something about possessing a proof of their crime. I don't know how plausible it is that the same person pursued Sarah in New York and here.

We also don't know how reliable Monsieur Bonnard's statement is, and whether he had other motives."

Vega felt disappointed and somehow let down by the inspector's last comment. She had found the tobacconist/part-time librarian likeable and it would never have occurred to her to mistrust his words. "That's because I am an amateur", she told herself. "How stupid to let my emotions color my judgment." Her intuition had told her that she could trust Jean. But her intuition had failed before.

"We don't know how reliable Gary's statements are either," she interjected stubbornly.

"That's true. Theoretically Gary is a suspect too and could have a motive to lie or even to follow Sarah here to Europe. We'll check his travel records, but I doubt that he came to Strasbourg to kill Sarah. He could have done that much more easily while she was staying with him in Brooklyn. But we have to follow all the leads, especially the people she talked to on her cell phone in the days before she died," the inspector said and smiled indulgently.

The *Gaststube* had calmed down and most of the guests had returned to either their jobs or to a siesta. Mme. Merrier wiped her hands on the blue apron that stretched tightly over her considerable bust. She sat down next to the inspector with a smile.

"May I tempt you with dessert?" she asked. "I baked rhubarb cake this morning. I think it is still warm." Looking in Vega's direction she added casually: "Any news about the Cinderella of the Mont Ste Odile?" Vega and the inspector both smiled.

"Is that what people call her around here?"

"She did loose her slipper, even though things must have gone awfully wrong with Prince Charming." Mme. Merrier's joke did not go over well with either of her guests.

"Nothing promising, just a lot of confusing and vague leads," the inspector said for both of them.

Mme. Merrier just smiled like the Cheshire cat

"I'll take four pieces of your rhubarb cake home with me. We'll have them this afternoon," Vega said, eager to change the subject, and also because her husband and children adored Mme. Merrier's rhubarb cake.

Saturday, May 23, 9 AM, Strasbourg:

Sergeant Mallarmé was in a bad mood as he walked along the Rue des Grandes Arcades toward the Place du Temple Neuf. The chestnut trees overhead were full of robins, starlings, and blackbirds singing their hearts out, outdoing each other in their welcoming song to spring. The fresh green leaves cast a pleasant shadow on the broad boulevard, and the mild air smelled of daffodils and lilacs.

"It's just my luck to be on weekend duty on a day like this!" Mallarmé mumbled under his breath. His wife and children were probably already sitting under a shady tree in the park, or playing ball, and later they would go to lunch at his parents' house and sit at the long table out on the porch. He better stop thinking about it and concentrate on his task ahead, or else he'd go crazy just imagining the fresh leg of lamb his mother would surely have in the oven by now. He looked up angrily at the birds above.

"What are they all singing about?" he muttered, shaking his head. He was not looking forward to this assignment. Why did he have to talk to that ghastly landlady again? What was her name? Gluck something. Why couldn't the inspector do that himself, if it was so important? And then he had to talk to her "guests" in the boarding house again. What a bunch of losers! They had already been interviewed about the dead girl. The reports lay typed and filed on the inspector's desk. Nobody had seen anything, they had passed the victim on the stairs, mumbled *bonjour*, and that was the extent of their interaction! Couldn't the inspector read? There were new developments, he had said. As if that would make a difference to those kinds of people. Didn't he know the type? Even if they had seen a man with a bloody knife bursting out of the victim's bedroom, would they tell the police anything? No, in their eyes the police was just a bunch of flicks. And now he would have the pleasure of spending a good part of a perfectly gorgeous Saturday morning in their rotten company. Without noticing, Mallarmé had arrived at Rue de l'Outre Number 13. He looked across the plaza, blinking into the sun and decided to talk to the tobacco storeowner, Jean Bonnard, first.

After crossing under the chestnut trees he realized that the store was still closed. Fortunately the owner lived in the apartment right above his business. Mallarmé pressed the doorbell long and hard. A disheveled head poked out of a window above.

"Who is it?" he asked sleepily.

"Sergeant Mallarmé, police. I have a few questions."

"Do you know what time it is? It's Saturday morning!" protested the head of Bonnard.

"I am well aware which day of the week it is," Mallarmé retorted bitterly. "This is important."

"Come on up then." The head disappeared with a sigh, and the intercom buzzed Mallarmé into the lobby of the turn-of-the century building. He followed a graceful staircase with polished mahogany banisters to the second floor, where Jean Bonnard stood in a crumpled T-shirt and shorts.

"Excuse the casual attire, but I wasn't expecting visitors," he said sarcastically as he stepped aside and let the policeman enter. Mallarmé took in the spacious apartment with its modern steel and leather furniture and light carpets. Some of the prints and paintings on the wall looked familiar to him, even though he was not exactly the art expert, especially when it came to modern stuff that didn't even look like anything anymore. He sat down on an elegant and fragile-looking wire chair and found it surprisingly comfortable.

"Coffee?" his host asked and he accepted gratefully.

"To what do I owe the honor of this visit, then?" Jean asked from the kitchen counter that abutted the living room.

"A man with a blue BMW," Mallarmé answered bluntly.

"Yes, of course." He brought over two cups of steaming coffee and a little jar of milk.

"Could you tell us everything you know about him - description, time, how often you saw him?" prompted Mallarmé while he took a sip from his cup.

"I saw him once or twice, across the plaza, through the store window. I did not get a good look. Then I saw Sarah getting into the car with him and they drove off."

"When was this? Which day?" asked Mallarmé sharply.

"I don't know, I don't remember. I did not write it in my diary," Bonnard answered irritably.

"It's very important. Try to remember. What time of day was it?"

"It was in the afternoon, I was in the store and the sun was low, so it must have been around four or four thirty. I think it was maybe three weeks ago?" he said vaguely.

"What was she wearing?"

"She wore a black miniskirt and a pink leather jacket, I think" Mallarmé took note in his notebook and also had the tape recorder running. He'd have to check if this description matched with the outfit Sarah wore when she died.

"What did he wear?"

"A blue suit. Sunglasses. I could not see very well from the distance."

"Why didn't you tell us about this man in the first interview we had? And why didn't you come forward with this information earlier?"

Jean scratched his head and screwed up his face. "It didn't seem important, and frankly, I simply didn't think of it."

"Monsieur Bonnard, you have not been quite forthright with us."

"What do you mean? I just forgot about this incident."

"You also haven't told us about your previous conviction."

"It was an accident. I have paid for it, believe me!"

"Monsieur Bonnard, where were you in the night from May eleven to twelve?"

"So now I am a suspect?" Jean jumped up from the sofa in indignation. "Just because twenty years ago I was involved in a fatal accident?"

"Just answer the question, please." Mallarmé was all business now.

"I was here. I was sleeping," he said resignedly.

"You are sure about that? It is after all almost two weeks ago and you did not even have to think?" Mallarmé was suspicious now.

"Look, I don't have a great social life. I work, I have coffee or a drink with friends, but at nights I mostly read right here at home. I know that does not sound exciting and probably does not fit into your profile, but that's the way my life is."

"Any witnesses?"

"Do you see any witnesses around? I live alone. I don't even have a cat; the landlord won't allow it. I am a bachelor."

"Did you have a relationship with the victim?"

"No. I think I would have been interested, but she was not receptive. We had coffee and lunch once in a while."

"This man in the blue BMW, is he real, or did you just make him up to shift attention away from you? So we would be searching for a 'phantom', instead of suspecting you?"

"This is enough. This interview is over. I am not saying another word to you."

"That is probably wise, because whatever you say could be used against you," Mallarmé concluded and packed up his tape recorder and notebook.

"Thanks for the coffee. I'll see myself out." He left his host crumpled on the sofa, shaking his head in disbelief.

"Just turning up the heat," thought Mallarmé on his way down the stairs. "He is a liar, that much we know, so why shouldn't he have lied about other facts as well?" Bonacourt would be pleased, he kept thinking, but somehow he did not feel very proud of himself.

Mallarmé pondered the more unpleasant task still before him as he once again crossed the plaza toward Number 13. There was nothing else to do but get it over with. He pushed the doorbell, which rang shrilly through the hallway inside.

"Who is it?" demanded the piercing voice of the landlady though the intercom.

"Police!" bellowed Mallarmé into the static of the intercom.

"What do you lot want here again! Haven't you caused enough damage? How many times do we have to tell you, this is a respectable house…"

Mallarmé winced at the not unexpected onslaught and entered the sour smelling lobby after the buzzer had released the heavy glass door. Immediately he was confronted by the lady of the house in all her formidable fury.

"If I see you lot here one more time I am going to file a formal complaint. This is a respectable house, we have no business with the police. My tenants have a right to their privacy and don't need to be disturbed and insulted on a Saturday morning, at a completely inappropriate time…"

"*Bonjour* to you too, Madame Gluck," Mallarmé said pleasantly. "Have you seen a man with a blue BMW around here?" he quickly added. "Middle aged, sunglasses good suits? He came to fetch Sarah Parker?"

Mme. Gluck was momentarily taken aback, which was such an unusual sight that it gave Sergeant Mallarmé a short moment of pleasure seeing her rendered temporarily speechless. Unfortunately she recovered quickly.

"I've told that other fellow, what's his name, the one with the walrus mustache, over and over again that she was cavorting with unsavory company and that it was no wonder she came to a bad end, but does anybody listen to me? I want to die in my bed, so I stay away from suspicious company. But would she listen, did the other policeman listen? How many times do I have to repeat myself? It's the same with my tenants; I tell them, wipe your feet before you walk onto the carpet, don't keep the water running, but do they listen? No, it's worse than with children I tell you—"

"Madame Gluck, the 'unsavory company', as you call it, was that a man in a blue BMW with German number plates?" Mallarmé interrupted the gush.

"Where did they find you? Are you deaf? Do I have to spell it out in capital letters? That's what I end up doing with the tenants. Look at all the signs everywhere, WIPE YOUR FEET, it's like a kindergarten, I tell you, but what can I do? I talk and talk all day, but it doesn't make any difference, so I write it up and hang the papers everywhere, so they can't avoid them, hoping they can at least read, and now you need me to write it all down for you too?"

"Actually, that would be a good idea, if you can make a signed statement that you have seen a man driving a blue BMW repeatedly coming to this house and picking up Sarah Parker. A description of the man would also be very helpful," Mallarmé stated with as much dignity as he could muster, considering that they were still standing in the narrow lobby behind the entrance door under a neon light fixture and Mme. Gluck had been screaming into his ear at close distance for about eight minutes now.

"I'm not signing anything! You must be out of your mind. First you come here and disturb a poor woman's peace on a Saturday morning, now you want me to sign something? I already told you what I know, so you can at least leave law-abiding citizens in peace, you hear me? There was the lad with the ponytail and then there was the other man. He was burly, taller than you, broader, he had good suits on, and he looked like a businessman. At first I was surprised, I thought, 'Where did she find him?' But mind you he wasn't the only one."

"We will send a police artist to make a drawing according to your description."

"I don't need an artist in my house. They are all the same, nothing but trouble. I've had my share of artists, I tell you. They make a mess, they are up all night, they have no money. I've learned my lesson the hard way, no more artists in this house; I make sure of that before I rent out a room."

"Madame Gluck, this is a police officer, who draws profiles of suspects; I promise you he won't make a mess. We just want to know what this gentleman, who came calling for Sarah Parker, looked like."

"She had all kinds of gentleman friends; I had to tell her to meet them somewhere else. I didn't want her sleazy business in my house! I have a reputation to uphold!"

"But we are talking about a specific man who came here in a blue BMW repeatedly to pick up Sarah Parker shortly before her death, correct? Did he have a name, this man?" Mallarmé was sweating in his uniform under the light fixture, taking notes, trying to keep the resemblance of a coherent story, since all his hopes for a signed statement had vanished.

"I never said anything about repeated visits. I opened the door for him once, and I spoke with him nicely, because I have manners. I've been brought up well, not like this lot nowadays who doesn't know how to look a person in the eye and say *bonjour*! When he answered I noticed that he did not speak

French very well, so I switched to German. I am an educated woman, you see, I can speak German as well as French. I said, 'What can I do for you, monsieur?' And he said 'I am here for Sarah Parker, what is her room number?' So, I said 'Who should I say is calling?' Because in my house nobody can just walk in from the street and go to the guest rooms, we need to follow a few rules here, or else all we have is chaos. Then he said, 'Can you give her this message?' And he gave me this note. I said 'I don't even know if she is in right now, but I will get this to her,' and he said 'thank you' and then he left. The whole time he kept his sunglasses on, even though it was nighttime, and he had this slicked back brown hair, like plastered to his head. I thought, 'This is no ordinary businessman,' not what I thought at first. Sarah was not expecting him, she was not even in, and when I gave her the message, she turned pale as a sheet. Not that she had much color in her cheeks normally, mind you."

"He did not give any name, did he?" asked Mallarmé faintly.

"You are deaf, aren't you? Didn't I just tell it to you, in every detail, what he said, what I said, and you standing there taking notes, and in the end you still don't remember what I said? Must be your brains are all softened up from television and such," she concluded utterly disgusted.

"Right," muttered Mallarmé, "what did the note say?" he asked harmlessly, figuring it may just slip her tongue, because he was absolutely certain that she had read the note. But he had no such luck.

"What do you take me for? A sneak, an old busybody? You think I read letters for my guests? There is such a thing as trust and privacy and integrity, even if you have never heard of it!"

"Yes, well, I still have to speak to the other tenants again."

"You think they know more than me? You think they can tell you his name and address?" Mallarmé knew better than to answer these questions and quietly ascended the stairs to the second floor, passing numerous signs telling him to wipe his feet. He knew from the file that only two boarders at Mme. Gluck's pension had overlapped with Sarah's stay there: Matt Taylor, an American student attending language classes in Strasbourg, and Vivian Vetter, a German history student who wrote her thesis about the Strasbourg Münster's astronomical clock and the interface of religion and science in the Renaissance. Without any assistance, and without hindrance by Mme. Gluck, Mallarmé made his way upstairs to Vivian Vetter's room and knocked.

He heard soft music playing, probably something baroque, Bach or Vivaldi, and a moment later the door opened and Vivian stood in front of him, red spiky hair glowing orange in the morning sun, cigarette in hand, and golden nose ring gleaming.

"What is it?" she asked slightly annoyed, looking at his uniform.

"May I please have a word with you?" he responded politely, hoping not to get off on the wrong foot with her as well. "It's about Sarah Parker."

"Alright, come in, but I already told the other inspector all I know."

She stepped aside and Mallarmé entered the room, which was brighter and more spacious than he had expected. Three tall windows looked out onto the Place du Temple Neuf and the morning sunlight filtered through the green chestnut leaves. Vivian had moved the small table in front of the window and had obviously been working there, because it was cluttered with papers.

"It is about a man with a blue BMW who was seen picking up Sarah Parker from this pension. Did you ever see him, or did she talk to you about him?" asked Mallarmé awkwardly. He stood in the middle of the room, because the only chair was pushed in at the desk and he did not want to sit down on the still unmade bed. Vivian ignored his discomfort and sat down in her chair sideways, dangling her bare legs in a supremely relaxed fashion and faced him with an amused expression.

"Ah, the blue phantom!" she exclaimed taking a deep drag of her cigarette. Mallarmé secretly wondered if Mme. Gluck approved of smoking in her guest rooms, but from Vivian's demeanor he surmised even someone of Mme. Gluck's caliber could not easily deter her.

"Who?" he asked, opening his notebook and readying his pen.

"The man we called the 'phantom', if that's who you are referring to." Mallarmé looked up in surprise as the words he had said just an hour ago to the tobacco store owner, were repeated back to him.

"Mademoiselle, please be more specific. Did Sarah speak to you about a man pursuing her, who drove a blue BMW with German number plates?"

"She spoke about a man pursuing her, yes. He had been hunting her for years, and she thought he had found her again here."

"What was the nature of your relationship with Sarah Parker?"

"Our rooms were next to each other. We were both German, we talked sometimes and had a cigarette together. I helped her with a couple of jobs, guiding German tourists through Strasbourg. I gave them my spiel about the astronomical clock. I only came here a couple of months ago, so that's how long I knew her, but look, I've told all that to the other fellow."

"I know, but we are now focusing in on the 'phantom' as you call him. Could you give us a description?"

"I never saw him. I even doubted he existed. I liked Sarah, but she was messed up. You couldn't be sure what was real or not with her. When she spoke about being haunted by the phantom, I told her to turn it around. Confront him, I said. Don't just hide and run."

"Did she take your advice?" asked Mallarmé, thinking that a confrontation might have led to Sarah's death.

"I don't know. She was thinking about it. She seemed surprised when I mentioned it; apparently she had never considered that option herself," Vivian said with a contemptuous snort.

"Did she ever tell you why he was chasing her?"

"Something to do with her childhood and her father. Her father was dead, and she felt it was somehow her fault and this fellow was connected to his death."

"How was her father's death her fault?"

"She thought that she had set him up somehow."

"Did the phantom have a name?"

"No, he wouldn't be a phantom otherwise, would he?" said Vivian, shuffling her papers and flicking the ash of her cigarette out of the window with a careless gesture.

"How was Sarah supposed to confront him?"

"Tell him to leave her alone, tell him he had nothing to fear from her, tell him if he didn't stop, she would go to the police. It was making her sick, all that fear and hiding."

"Do you know when this confrontation was going to take place?"

"No, I don't even know whether it ever did take place. I didn't have a chance to ask Sarah, because she was dead by the time I came back from Germany."

"You weren't here when she was murdered?"

"I went to see my family for a week and made a presentation at my university. When I came back she was dead."

It was a good alibi, Mallarmé thought.

"Look, I really do have some work to do. I think that's all I can tell you."

"Thank you, mademoiselle, I won't take any more of your time."

Mallarmé grabbed his notebook and left. The American boarder, Matt Taylor was just getting up as Mallarmé knocked on door # 7. He remembered that Taylor had never exchanged more than a greeting with Sarah Parker. He might have seen the BMW though, thought Mallarmé as he entered the messy and stuffy room.

The young American let him in and then sat sullenly on the unmade bed leaving the hard backed wooden chair to Mallarmé, who wondered about the difference between this room and the one he had just visited. They were just right next to each other, sparsely furnished with the same few items, but while Vivian's room was light and bright and had colorful prints on the walls, this room looked neglected and gloomy, with its drawn curtains and tightly closed windows. Its occupant blinked at Mallarmé as if even the dimmed interior was painful to his eyes.

"I was out late last night," he explained, "drinking with a few buddies from Texas. I think I need to take an aspirin." Mallarmé allowed him to rummage around in the small bathroom, and the young man returned with a half-drunk glass of water.

"You are here attending language school, correct?" Mallarmé opened the conversation.

"Yes, and I am not happy about it. What am I going to need French conversation skills for? I am going back to Texas as soon as possible, and I am going to stay there. Nobody speaks French in Dallas!" he spoke in broken French.

"It was your parents' idea, I gather?"

"They thought I needed some European exposure - different lifestyles, all that crap."

He suddenly switched to English, which Mallarmé followed with difficulties.

"My lifestyle at home is just fine and dandy, thank you very much! I don't need cream sauce dinners and French wine expertise. I like beer better anyway."

Mallarmé nodded and tried to bring the conversation back on target.

"Did you ever see a man with a blue BMW in front of or inside this house?"

"Is this something to do with that Sarah Parker girl again?" he retorted contemptuously. "She was an arrogant bitch."

Mallarmé flinched at the coarse expression; even with his limited English, he knew this was no way to talk about a girl, let alone a dead one.

"Why would you say that?" he asked evenly, trying to understand Taylor's anger.

"She thought she was better than everybody else. She didn't have that much going for her, scraping by on guiding tours. Pretty pitiful existence, if you ask me."

"Did you have any social contact with her? Go for a drink or something?" Mallarmé asked harmlessly.

"No. I asked her if she wanted to go and have a beer with me, but she was above that. Said she didn't drink beer. I said, 'You can drink something else if you like,' but she just smiled in this really patronizing way, almost sadly, as if she felt sorry for me, and shook her head. I mean, I felt humiliated. That's the last time I ever spoke to her."

"When was that?" Mallarmé took notes feverishly.

"Oh, a few weeks ago, in the beginning of May probably."

"About two weeks before Sarah's death," thought Mallarmé. This statement contradicted Taylor's earlier version about never exchanging more than a *bonjour* on the stairs with Sarah. Would a grudge like this be enough to physically harm a girl, he wondered. *Never discount anything*, echoed Bonacourt's words in his mind, and he made a mental note to emphasize it in his report.

"The man with the blue BMW?" Mallarmé reminded the young American.

"Can't say I remember seeing him. I leave early and usually return late. This is not exactly a cozy place to come home to. I stay out as much as possible."

"You have been here for a couple of months, haven't you? Why didn't you try to find another lodging?" asked Mallarmé.

Matt ruffled his short brown hair and shook his head. "It's cheap and convenient here. I am not going to settle in and move here or anything. I am going back in three weeks; my time's up."

"I am sorry you did not enjoy your stay here," said Mallarmé, feeling suddenly protective of his hometown.

"Well, it's just not my thing. But hey, to each his own." He got up and opened the door for Mallarmé, the interview obviously concluded.

As Mallarmé walked down the stairs, he hoped that he would not have to come back to this inhospitable place again ever. He gladly let the heavy glass door click into the lock behind him and breathed deeply the fresh spring air in the Place du Temple Neuf. Across the plaza he saw the tobacco store, now open. Apparently others had seen the phantom, and it had not just been a figment of Jean Bonnard's imagination. He felt he owed the owner something of an apology. He would think about it after lunch. Maybe his report could wait until he had stopped by his parents' house for a bite to eat with his family.

Sunday, May 24, 10 AM, Hagenau:

M. Bonacourt sat in his office in shirtsleeves with the window wide open. Those were the only concessions he made to a beautiful spring Sunday. Other than that, he had come to work as usual, weekend or not, and now sat reading translations of Sarah Parker's letters.

> *New York, January 15*
> *Dear Karl,*
> *I am glad the holidays are over and things are returning to*
> *normal, even though I am not sure what normal is anymore,*
> *at least for me. I've been helping Gary again, not every day,*
> *but once in a while to make some money, but also because he*
> *is a good guy. He should not be wasting his time with me! He*
> *says he enjoys spending time together with me. He sometimes*
> *reminds me of you, Karl. So calm and patient. Last Sunday*
> *we did a real New York kind of thing. We took a taxi cab*
> *(Gary knows I hate subways) uptown to Central Park and*
> *we walked between the barren trees in the frosty air under a*
> *gray white sky. Few people were out, it was bitter cold and the*
> *snow looked ashen from the pollution, but a few brave souls*

turned circles on the ice skating rink. Gary took pictures of the trees (his favorite subject, apparently) and then we rushed over to 53rd Street to the Museum of Modern Art. Gary wanted to see some photography exhibit, and I mainly wanted to get out of the cold. Suddenly I saw this picture by Picasso, called the "Demoiselles d'Avignon". It's really large and Gary says its one of the most famous paintings in the world. Needless to say, I had never seen it before, not even in a book. But I really understand why it is so famous. Because the women in the painting are all fragmented, as if someone had cut them apart and then put them together again in the wrong order. They still look very much alive but somehow trapped in these bizarre constellations. One in the background has a very dark face, more like a mask, but to me, she just could not hide her dark side anymore and it just became visible one day. The woman in front of her is really distorted, her body is flayed and one eye is bright and white and looks directly at you, while the other is dark blue and strangely slanted and it somehow does not seem to be able to focus as well as the other eye. Half of her face is in darkness, starting at the viciously sharp nose. She is still in the transition period, where her dark and her light side are battling it out, and you are not sure who will win, even though judging from the others and the tortured position of her body, I would bet the dark side wins.

I told Gary a little about these thoughts and he said he had never looked at it that way, although I find it quite obvious.

I could really relate to this painting. I feel like that many times: fragmented, disconnected, damaged, contorted, battling with the dark side that wants to take over. I must say, Picasso was a pretty amazing artist to be able to capture all that. No wonder people make such a big deal about him.

Gary said that Picasso was not very nice to women, but I think he just painted what he felt about their souls. I hope it's not too late for mine.

I look forward to seeing you in the spring for your wedding!

Your loving, freezing sister,

Sarah

Bonacourt looked out the open window to the fresh green leaves of the chestnut tree, which stood tall enough to shade part of his second story office. The smell of cut grass, a gentle breeze and the exuberant songs of starlings drifted in. Bonacourt barely noticed. He got up and moved some piles of books from one chair to another, until he found what he was looking for. He opened his old art history text book to the page displaying the famous painting by Picasso and glanced at it for a minute. "Sarah was a very tortured soul," he thought, judging from the faces of Picasso's demoiselles.

New York, February 14

Dear Karl,

Well it looks like I am going to come back to Germany earlier than planned. Again I did not get away far enough, and my curse has caught up with me. I thought 'This time I'll be able to disappear in the masses of New York. He won't bother coming after me all this way'. But he has. I know what he wants from me, why he pursues me so relentlessly. But I won't give it to him. Dad died for this secret and I won't betray him.

Spring of Tears

I am writing this letter in a coffee shop in Brooklyn. I don't dare go back to my hotel. Last night when I came home, I walked through the alleyway behind Spring Street and suddenly he came at me out of the shadows. He is big and he is pretty strong. He pinned me to the wall of a building and started choking me. Give me the picture, he kept saying. I said, 'I don't know what you are talking about'. Then he started beating me slapping my face and my arms. He kept saying, 'You and your father just don't know what's good for you!'

My nose started to bleed, and I could feel the bruises on my arm. I screamed and he clamped his hand on my mouth. I still could not see him very well, he had a black leather cap with a rim on and was dressed all in black. The commotion had alerted some people, and they were coming into the alley and starting to shout, 'What's going on?' and he pushed me to the ground and hissed at me, 'You are just a dirty, little rat and you better remember what happens to rats when they cross my path!' Of course I remember the rat with its severed head in front of my bed in Brooklyn!

Then he walked away quickly. I was shaking and bleeding and I turned around to the subway and rode to Brooklyn and knocked on Gary's window. I did not know where else to go. He let me sleep there for the night on his couch, but I can't stay. I cannot endanger him. Karl, I hate to do this to you, but please book a ticket for me back to Germany. I'll fax this to your office and you can respond to the same number. It's Gary's. Or you can call me and tell me which airline and time and I'll just go to the airport and wait

there. I cannot stay here any longer. I'll make it up to you, I
promise! Please Karl, this one last time.
Your shaken sister,
Sarah

Bonacourt felt little beads of sweat on his arms and neck. He did not know whether the warm sunshine or the grim report form New York had caused them. He read on.

Airspace over the Atlantic Ocean, February 15
Dear Karl,
I am writing this letter on the flight from New York to
Frankfurt. Soon I will see you again in person, but I feel the
need to write this letter anyway. I don't know how much
opportunity we'll have to talk, with Leah there and your
wedding coming up. Karl, once again you saved me. I wish I
could reciprocate for once, or at least prove myself worthy of all
your help! Thank you for booking this flight home for me. I
wish this excursion to New York had ended more favorably.
It started out so promising. I don't know when things started
to spiral out of control. Of course they always spiral
downward - never up. Of course drugs had to do with it. But
I was so afraid that I needed drugs to calm me down. All in
all, it could have turned out even worse. I could have ended up
dead, instead of flying back to Germany.

What a wedding present for you! Leah must hate
me, taking up your time and money right before your big day.
I am so sorry! I don't know how many times you can say
you're sorry until it becomes mute. I still mean it, and I still

want to change and make a new start. I know I can do it as
long as I feel safe. Don't give up on me yet, Karl. Remember
when we were children, and Mom would fly into one of her
fits, we would stick together and hide under the table together
until she was done screaming? We always helped each other,
and you still do. I wish I could do something for you as well.
Maybe one day I will. That is my goal, that's what keeps me
going.
Your remorseful sister,
Sarah

"How tragic", Bonacourt thought. Sarah had made it safely back to Europe only to be murdered there. "What went wrong?"

Tübingen, March 2, 2001
Dear Karl,
I am writing this letter to you from the spot where the willows
dip into the Neckar right by the Hölderlin Turm and create a
green room on the banks, where you can hide from the sun
and the world, sheltered by bright green branches and gently
lapping water! Remember how we used to come here to sit and
talk?

Your wedding was beautiful, and Leah seems very
nice. Very different from what I had expected. She is so dark
and passionate, almost irrational, the total opposite of you.
But that's probably the attraction. She seems warm and
clearly loves you very much. Will she still be your student, now
that you are married?

I had a good time at your reception in the Garden Restaurant Schwärzloch with all the peacocks walking around! It has been a long time since I ate Zwiebelkuchen and drank Moscht! It really felt like I had come home. It can be so comforting to eat the foods of your childhood.

You seem so at ease and established and well respected. I am so proud of you! You deserve all the happiness coming your way! Thank you for letting me be a part of this special day, even though I did not contribute very much. I am working hard on stabilizing my mind and body. Now I just need to find something to fill the big emptiness inside of me. It's like a giant gaping hole, screaming for drugs and threatening to swallow all happiness and everything that belongs to me. I feel the need for something spiritual and you know it can't be the Christian religion. I am reading a good book, Hermann Hesse's, 'Siddhartha'. Did you ever read that one? It helps me fill my mind with good thoughts. I'll also try Nietzsche again, but I need our conversations to make sense of him.

Here is a quote from Hesse that I read sitting by the Neckar: 'The river has many voices. The voice of a king and a warrior, a bull and a night owl. All the voices of the creatures are in the river, if you can hear all 10,000 of them at the same time, then the river speaks to you.' Hesse wrote this book about a holy man in India. I think I will travel to India on my quest for meaning. My little pension from Dad would go much further there, and I'd be safe. I don't want to get on your nerves, and Leah and you need some privacy now, so you can really get to know each other. I just need to get to

know myself better, and I think I can do that in India.

Hopefully soon I can repay you for all your kindness!

Love, Your recovering sister,

Sarah

Sarah had really covered some ground. From New York via Tübingen to India. "She led an interesting life," Bonacourt thought, even though it did not sound like she enjoyed it much. However, he was curious to read what transpired in India. Could anybody possibly have pursued her there?

Goa, Calangute Beach, India, June 22

Dear Karl,

I finally completed a crazy and exhausting journey, which is

the reason I didn't write earlier. I got out of Bombay as soon

as possible; it was noisy and hot. But now I have arrived at a

beautiful and peaceful place. You would love it. Remember

what I wrote to you about the many voices of the river in

Hermann Hesse's "Siddhartha"? Well, I rented a little house

right next to a river! The river is shallow and the house is

very small. It does not have running water, but there is a well

right outside, and it has a big veranda where I sit at nights

and in the afternoon to look out onto the river and watch it

change. The river wears many different colored clothes: tender

pink in the morning, gold in the afternoon, deep green or

azure blue before noon, and black at night. If you manage to

see all its colors at once, then you see nothing. The river is

clear and transparent, but it reflects all life around it. It has

many functions, it's a place for washing for the women, and

the men catch fish in it by walking shoulder deep in the water,
with a big net between them. The river also gives the ferryman
a job, because it has no bridge. If the water is low, I can wade
across, because my house is on the other side, but if the water
is high, the ferryman stands next to his outrigger boat made of
two palm trunks and takes me across for 10 rupies (about 2
pennies). He takes bicycles, people, bricks, and coconuts
across. Everybody knows the price and pays, if not this time
then the next. The ferryman's face never shows an expression
under the brown hood of his robe. The river is like a ribbon, a
street, and a dividing line. It is the stage for the nightly
spectacle of the sunset, for which everybody dresses up and
secures a good seat. The locals have prime seats on the rocks
overlooking the ocean. Every night we attend and see an old
Indian man with a flowing beard sitting on top of the hill, a
dog at his side. The sunset dyes the sky, and the sky colors the
river purple, red, yellow, and orange. By the time the sun has
dipped into the blood red ocean the old man is gone.

Hesse writes: "The River teaches that there is no
time, because it is everywhere at once: at the origin and at the
delta, at the waterfall and at the ferry landing, at the rapids,
in the ocean, and in the mountains. For the river only the
present exists, not shadow or the past or future."
I am learning more from the river than from all my teachers
in High school. I hope you don't think me a fool, Karl,
because I know you are so much smarter than me. But I feel
very happy and safe here, and at home in a strange way.
Your loving sister,
Sarah

"So she had found a safe spot at last," Bonacourt thought, "in India of all places." Bonacourt himself had never had the desire to go to India, but he frequently dreamed of California's Big Sur coast, and how he might one day stay there for an extended time. He imagined himself spending hours gazing out onto the Pacific Ocean from the dramatic coastline. He returned from his reverie to the next letter in front of him.

Katmandu, May 10

Dear Karl,

Congratulations! You are a father! How exciting! I can't believe my little brother is all grown up, married, and has a child of his own! Wow! That means I am an aunt now! A title I always wanted. This baby of yours will give my life a whole new meaning. It is even worth coming back from India for! Before leaving Asia, I wanted to see the Himalayan Mountains. I loved India, but here in Nepal, I feel like I finally woke up to see the world as it really is. All the colors and outlines are so clear and intense in the thin mountain air. People are Buddhist and they seem so awake and clear-minded. I have bought an amazing piece of art, a roll painting of the Buddhist Wheel of Life. I hope it will remind me how caught up I was in my own little hell. I hope it will remind me to look at my life from a larger perspective: as if looking at it from the top of a mountain. It suddenly all seems quite small and unimportant. I used to feel such emptiness in my life; like a huge gaping hole in my soul. You found your answers in philosophy, and I filled my needs with drugs. That has all changed now. I think a baby gives you the chance to make a fresh start, to put right what has gone wrong before. I have decided to come back and settle in Strasbourg. I can work as a tour guide for German visitors. I'll be close enough to visit you and my little niece! It's not quite Germany, where I do not want to live anymore, but I'll be right at the border. It's far enough, I hope, far enough not to create any conflict with Leah. I understand that she is very critical of me and thinks I am just taking advantage of you. She is trying to protect you, and she has already seen a very dark side of me, so I don't blame her for not trusting me. But you, Karl, do you trust me? I need your approval more than anything in this world. Don't give up on me, please. I won't mess up; I'll make it work this time. Please say that you believe me!

Your hopeful sister,

Sarah

Here the letters ended. Bonacourt stared out of the window at the spring sky without seeing the puffy white clouds drifting by lazily. Sarah Parker's hopeful expectations had not come true. Was the man who attacked her in New York, the same man who had eventually killed her on the Mont Ste Odile? Bonacourt was not sure if the letters he just read would be in any way helpful in his investigation. He did not really want to delve into the sadness of Sarah's life on a beautiful Sunday in May, but what else could he do? Work was all he knew. Since his divorce, staying in his house at the outskirts of Strasbourg during the weekends had become difficult to bear. Whenever he walked out into his now neglected garden or sat on the vine-covered porch, memories from sitting there with his wife, Marie, drinking a choice Alsatian wine and looking at the fading light of the day, flooded his mind. Marie had always asked about his day in her calm and truly interested tone, and he had told her.

By talking to her, connections and events had become clearer in his own mind, and he felt calm and in control by the time the light had faded and they went indoors for the supper she had prepared. But there had been too many times when the supper had gotten cold and the wine remained un-drunk, because he had been called to a case or was retained at the police station, long beyond Marie's bedtime. Finally she had found someone else to share her evenings with, someone in academics, who worked regular hours and had long summer vacations. She had left him the house, but he really didn't want to spend time there anymore. So he came to his office and worked. Sarah's letters provided background ambience about the case, and he had a better idea who she had been as a person, but he did not feel that they provided any evidence to lead them to her murderer.

He lit a cigar and moved on to Mallarmé's report about his interviews with Bonnard and the inhabitants of the boarding house. In contrast to the letters, this report opened up all kinds of questions. Did Jean Bonnard speak the truth? Were Mme. Gluck and Vivian Vetter's statements reliable? Was the 'phantom' as he now seemed to be called by everybody, in the blue BMW the murderer? Was he the same man who attacked her in New York? Looking for a blue BMW in Germany, where they were produced and where one person out of ten was a BMW or Mercedes Benz owner, would be worse than looking for a needle in a haystack. Bonacourt decided to approach the case from a different angle and return to the place of the crime. Why had the murder occurred on top of the Mont Ste Odile? Why not just in a back alley in Strasbourg, or on the outskirts, in the open countryside? Why had the murderer gone to so much trouble to drive up the switchbacks with the victim and then proceed in the dark on the slippery path down to the Spring of Tears? He grabbed his lightweight jacket and went downstairs to his vintage Citroen convertible, his pride and joy. He would take a drive to Mont

Ste Odile and talk to the hotel manager. He would keep the roof down and then consider stopping at the *Golden Swan* on his way back. Content with this plan, Bonacourt inserted a CD with a Debussy piano concerto into his player and enjoyed the ride.

Sunday, May 24, 11 AM, Mont Ste Odile:

The clerk at the Ste Odile Hotel reception desk, a young girl in her early twenties, had her hair pulled back in a messy bun. She felt very uncomfortable in the inspector's presence. She was just covering the Sunday shift to supplement her income as a biology student, but she really did not know anything. The inspector could come back in the morning or call the manager. No, nobody could leave the confines of the former convent after 10 PM. If you were in, you were in, if you were out you, you were out, unless you had major climbing equipment and could scale the twelve foot walls of the convent enclosure. At that point in the conversation, Bonacourt's cell phone rang and he went outside to take the call.

"What? Impossible? When? I'll be right there?"

The young clerk heard the Bonacourt's exclamations with a certain relief, because this obviously meant that the inspector was going to leave her alone and drive as fast as possible to whoever had summoned him. She was new at this job and did not want to get involved with the police. That had not been part of the job description. She was never going to sign up for Sunday duty anymore, even if it paid overtime.

Bonacourt was already on his way to the parking lots outside the gates. He almost ran, jacket flapping behind him. As fast as he safely could, he raced down the switchbacks of the mountain, passing the *Golden Swan* with a regretful but determined glance. He should call in Mallarmé, he thought, even though he deserved his day off, but they would need an investigative team, especially now with another murder on their hands.

Sunday, May 24, 11:30 AM, Strasbourg:

The normally quaint and peaceful Place du Temple Neuf was transformed into a beehive by the commotion a murder investigation always creates. Half the plaza was blocked off with yellow crime scene tape, five police cars stood in the middle of the road, several officers redirected the traffic, and an ambulance, its blue lights still flashing, stood at an odd angle to the building. Barriers had been erected to keep away the curious onlookers who had assembled, Sunday morning coffee cups still in hand. Bonacourt was waved through the checkpoint and quickly approached the building. Mallarmé was already on the scene.

"Thanks for getting here so quickly," Bonacourt acknowledged.

Mallarmé nodded grimly.

"It's not a pretty picture," he warned, "and to think that I just spoke to her yesterday. I told her we would send a police artist to draw a profile. She objected of course, but you have read the report, I am sure."

Mallarmé and Bonacourt climbed the stairs to Mme. Gluck's private living quarters.

"She told me yesterday that she wanted to die in her bed," Mallarmé added as they entered the chaotic bedroom.

"It seems like she got her wish. She was most likely stabbed in her bed in her sleep," Bonacourt replied thoughtfully.

"And then the murderer arranged her like this, leaning against the side of the bed her nightshirt pulled up over her thighs, bedspreads crumpled?" Mallarmé asked doubtfully. "Why not leave her where she was, in her bed?"

Bonacourt took in the scene. He saw an old fashioned bed with a curved headboard, bedspreads dragged partially to the floor. The murdered landlady half sat, half slumped on the floor, legs spread wide apart, her upper body propped up against the side of the bed. She wore an old-fashioned white nightgown, which was hitched up to her thighs and exposed the white, scrawny bare legs. Bloodstains discolored the white gown at the area of the heart, where she had been stabbed, as well as the carpet below her. The figure of the old woman was illuminated by the spotlights of the crime-scene photographer in stark contrast to the rest of the room, which remained dimmed by drawn curtains. The scene looked oddly familiar, Bonacourt thought, and he scanned his mind for the time and circumstances when he had seen the likeness of this dramatic pose. Was it the theater; the movies? Finally his mental spotlight reached the appropriate section of his memory.

"It's a famous picture, by Daumier I think," he exclaimed, and seeing Mallarmé's uncomprehending look, added "It's about a poor inhabitant in the eighteen hundreds in Paris, who was murdered in his sleep by government forces. This must be a statement by the murderer."

Bonacourt motioned to the crime scene photographer

"Could you take a picture from this angle right here, please?"

The photographer did so, while Mallarmé looked on perplexed.

"Are you saying we are dealing with an artistically insane killer, who arranged the body like a famous painting?" he asked.

"It's a print actually," Bonacourt confirmed. "Who found the body?"

"One of the tenants. She wanted to check out and Madame Gluck wasn't at her desk, it was getting later and later, so she came up here and found this."

"She is still here, waiting with the others I hope?" Bonacourt asked even though he knew Mallarmé had followed procedures.

"She is very impatient, as you can imagine. She was planning to catch a train this morning."

"I'll talk to her first. Of course, we need to talk to all the other tenants. Maybe one of them heard something. I want to speak with the two tenants who knew Sarah personally. The two murders are connected, I am sure of it."

"What makes you so sure of that?" asked Detective Garand from the Strasbourg homicide division, who had just strutted into the room. As usual, he was dressed impeccably in a light gray double-breasted suit over a powder blue linen shirt. He swept back his fine blond hair and stared at his colleague. The chief detective, head of the Strasbourg police force, and Bonacourt, *commisario generell* of Hagenau had met before, and it had not been an entirely positive experience for either one of them, to put it mildly.

"Oh well," thought Bonacourt, "now the turf wars begin."

"Detective Garand, how good to see you!" he exclaimed pleasantly and extended his hand toward the younger man, who took it hesitantly.

"Bonacourt, I know you've been investigating the dead girl up on the Mont Sainte Odile, but this murder happened right in the center of Strasbourg, way outside of your jurisdiction," he proclaimed.

"Yes, technically you are correct, but the two murders are closely linked. The dead girl, whose name was Sarah Parker, by the way, lived in this pension."

"She was not alone. There is a whole room full of tenants waiting downstairs as we speak. Probably a mere coincidence," Garand replied.

Mallarmé nodded. "But, it cannot be a coincidence that Madame Gluck got killed one day after speaking to me about the man in blue."

"You mean the 'phantom'?" the inspector corrected him.

"What are you talking about?" Garand interrupted.

"We are talking about the suspect, detective," explained Bonacourt mildly. "Madame Gluck was about to identify the suspect, when she met her untimely end."

"And why do you call him a 'phantom' if you are so close to an identification?" Garand demanded.

"Not so close anymore, now that our main witness is not longer with us," regretted Bonacourt.

"You should have acted a little bit faster and left it to the Metropolitan police force. But now it's too late for regrets."

"Tell you what, there are enough suspects and witnesses for all of us. I just want to interview three of the people waiting down there: Vivian Vetter, Matt Taylor and…"

"Jean Bonnard," Mallarmé suddenly blurted out, "he knows about art. He would have known that Daumier person you mentioned. You should see his apartment, full of all kinds of pictures. Several of them I have seen someplace, I just don't know where. I am sure they are famous, or else they would not look familiar to me."

"Now who in the world is Daumier?" asked Garand, completely confused.

"French artist, nineteenth century. His specialty was social criticism and political protest. Great printmaker," Bonacourt added nonchalantly. He turned to Mallarmé:

"I want to question Bonnard. Summon him. He can wait with the others. I want to see if anybody recognizes him."

"Bonnard?" Garand asked, thoroughly confused now. "Isn't he another dead artist?"

"Monsieur Garand," answered Bonacourt, pleasantly surprised, "you are absolutely correct. Pierre Bonnard was indeed another nineteenth century artist. In this case, however, we are dealing with Jean Bonnard, who is still alive and by profession the tobacconist on the corner of the Place du Temple Neuf."

"This is your typical irrelevant chatter, Bonacourt. I know in the country side people have time for idle talk, but we have a murder on our hands and need to act efficiently!"

"I couldn't agree with you more, Monsieur Garand.

"Were there any signs of forced entry?" he asked Mallarmé, who shook his head:

"No, whoever did this either had a key or was already in the building. The entrance door is very sturdy, as Madame Gluck was a security-conscious person. Nobody could have tampered with it without our noticing or the tenants hearing any noise."

"Whoever killed Sarah Parker also has her purse with her keys and papers," Bonacourt reminded his two colleagues. "We need to find out if anything is missing. Considering the chaos, it certainly looks like the killer was looking for something. Remember the condition of Sarah's room after her death? Someone had certainly gone through her things with a fine-toothed comb."

Mallarmé nodded. "The note Madame Gluck mentioned. The one she gave to Sarah. I am still convinced she read it, and if I assume that, the phantom probably assumed the same. He came back to silence her."

"Possibly, Mallarmé, but let's not jump to conclusions too quickly. If the 'phantom' is our man, then Madame Gluck was indeed the only one who got a good look at him, and it was in his interest to get rid of her."

"In the form of a painting - I mean print - or whatever?" Mallarmé seemed unable to wrap his mind around the gruesome arrangement.

"Cause of death?" Garand barked, shaking his head at the interchange between Mallarmé and Bonacourt, but determined to reaffirm his authority.

"Apparently a stab wound with a very sharp knife or dagger directly into the heart," the pathologist on the scene answered. "The killer had a steady hand, there are only two stab wounds. Death must have occurred instantly, monsieur."

"Any trace of the murder weapon?" Garand turned to the forensic team searching the scene.

"No, monsieur. We are looking for the knife or dagger. The perpetrator seems to have taken it with him."

Mallarmé made a note on his writing pad.

"Time of death?" Garand inquired.

The pathologist looked up frowning and answered: "Detective Garand, you know better than to ask me that question at this stage in the investigation. But if you want a rough estimate and if you promise not to quote me on this, I'd say, considering the rigor mortis, she died between two and four o'clock this morning."

Garand's head turned red at this criticism; the pathologist was a good twenty years older than he, had decades more experience in police work, and did not mind reminding people of that fact. Mallarmé, whose vanity was not affected, processed the information.

"Our killer is a night owl. Sarah Parker was murdered around the same time," he remarked.

"Are we absolutely sure it was a man, Mallarmé?" asked Bonacourt, as they entered the small kitchen and lounge area, where two vending machines offered sodas and snacks. The seven current tenants plus Jean Bonnard sat nervously around the two Formica tables on plastic chairs. Garand had agreed to divide them into two groups: Bonacourt and Mallarmé would talk to Vivian, Matt, Jean, and Ulla the young Swedish girl who found the body; Garand and his men would take the rest. Bonacourt used Mme. Gluck's tiny office behind the reception area to conduct the interviews.

Ulla was still in a shock and could not contribute much more to their investigation, except that the door to Mme. Gluck's private apartment of the third floor had been slightly ajar.

"I would not have entered, otherwise!" she repeated. She had never been inside the apartment before and therefore could not tell if anything was out of the ordinary. Bonacourt took her contact information and let her go.

Matt Taylor was apparently still hungover, supposedly from another night of drinking, and hadn't heard or seen anything. When Bonacourt reminded him of the man in the blue BMW, he snapped,

"She just went out with guys with money, that's what she did. Probably one of her boyfriends." He hadn't seen the man or in any case he didn't care and couldn't tell one from the other. *Bad attitude* Bonacourt wrote in his notes.

"Do we have to move out of here now?" was Matt Taylor's last question.

"Probably," Bonacourt answered, not willing to set the young man's mind at ease.

Vivian Vetter was visibly shaken by the event. She smoked one cigarette after the other, and Bonacourt thought he was going to choke in the stuffy, windowless little office.

"This is terrible, this kind of stuff isn't supposed to happen in real life. Things like this happen only in the movies or in mystery novels!" she exclaimed in indignation.

Bonacourt smiled. "I wish you were right. I would gladly be an inspector in a novel, with corpses made up of words on paper instead of flesh and blood. All the pain could just be a thrill for the reader before bedtime, and we could all disappear between the pages at the end of the story."

Despite herself Vivian seemed to get drawn into the imaginary tale: "We could write our own ending, and I prefer a happy one," she said.

"Help me bring this case, if not to a happy then at least to a just ending. I need to find who did this to Madame Gluck and Sarah." Bonacourt leaned forward and looked at Vivian intensely.

"You think it was the same man?" she recoiled to distance herself from the thought.

"There are striking similarities."

"What similarities?" Vivian asked sharply.

"I am not at liberty to say. You need to tell me everything you did last night, at what time did you go to bed, did you hear anything, and was there anything about Madame Gluck's behavior that was different?"

Vivian thought for a minute. "I went out to dinner last night, with a colleague from the university. We had a great meal at Ami Schulz, and then walked around Petit France. I got home around eleven, I read awhile and then went to sleep around midnight. I did not hear anything out of the ordinary. There are always noises in a boarding house like this. People come in late, like that American guy on the first floor. Mme. Gluck - she always made a big deal about this being a respectable house and tenants had to be home at ten, but it was not realistic and we had our own keys, so we could come home at any time. You asked, if Madame Gluck's behavior was different: Not that I noticed. She was in a bad mood, which was not unusual for her, especially on Saturday after your constable visited."

"Sergeant," Bonacourt corrected.

"You were one of her long-term tenants. Do you know if Madame Gluck had any friends, or visitors?"

"To be honest, I don't think that she had much talent for making friends. More like the opposite: She was good at making enemies." Vivian puffed on her cigarette and blew out a stream of smoke into the room, which suddenly made the faint rays of light coming in from the lobby visible like a hidden web of strings.

"I've been thinking about the questions your sergeant asked yesterday. My god, I can't believe it was only yesterday. It seems much longer. Anyway, I realized that everything Sarah said could be highly significant, especially in light of what happened to her and ... the landlady."

"And also dangerous," interjected the inspector. "That's why we have to move quickly. We changed the locks and will also place a guard in front of the pension and observe the entire plaza."

"I appreciate that. Here is what Sarah told me, and what I pieced together: Twenty-five years ago, Sarah's father attacked a priest. Sarah felt she was responsible for the assault, because her father went to confront the priest on her account." Vivian stubbed out her cigarette in a plastic ash tray and lit another one right away.

"As a result of the attack the priest was paralyzed, but Sarah's father was the real victim. You have heard how he died in prison three years later. But apparently, Sarah's father had taken a picture from the priest and gave it to Sarah with the instruction of safekeeping. This man chasing her, the phantom, he was in that picture. The picture incriminated him in some way, but Sarah did not know how. Her father said he needed time to collect more evidence, but the picture was proof of a crime he had discovered. Unfortunately he did not have time to explain the crime or collect the evidence, because he died shortly afterwards." Vivian wrinkled her nose concentrating.

"The man in the picture was never convicted and Sarah didn't know exactly what the crime had been. She knew it had to do with the photo, and that it was very important. That's what her pursuer was after. You see, when I told her to turn the game around, to confront the man who threatened her, she said, she couldn't because she did not know why the picture was so crucial and why it was incriminating. It was a vicious circle. I told her to just give him the picture and be done with it, after all these years. Sarah did not want to do that. It would have been a betrayal of her father's sacrifice, she said. 'Then bluff,' I told her, 'and pretend that you know more than you actually do. Threaten him with exposure'. But by giving her this advice - " Vivian faltered and her voice broke, "I am afraid that I may have sent her to her death."

Her shoulders shook and she started to sob quietly. "I tried to help, but I only made it so much worse! Now, two people are dead, possibly because of me."

Bonacourt handed her a large handkerchief and laid his hand on her shaking shoulder soothingly.

"If she really confronted him, it was her decision to do it," he objected. "She had been on the run for too long. It's all a matter of cause and effect. Sometimes it is hard to foresee what consequences our words and actions can have. And it can be difficult to live with them," Bonacourt admitted, avoiding cheap words of comfort. The young German girl would have to come to grips with the events she might have set into motion, and at the moment, he felt it was better if she felt a deep sense of responsibility and involvement. It would make her more willing to help and think about small details that might hold clues to solving the case.

"Did you ever see the photograph she mentioned?" asked Bonacourt.

"No, but it must have been with her things. Because of this picture her father went to jail, and she suffered for so many years. She said it was in a safe place and that after all the pain and suffering they had been through she was not going to give it up. You must have found it when you took all her things away."

"Someone, presumably the killer, searched the place after her death. Maybe he found it."

"But if he did, then why this second murder?" asked Vivian logically.

"Because Madame Gluck had presumably seen him. She was going to work with a police artist on a profile."

"How did the killer know that so quickly? It was only yesterday that your Sergeant talked to…you know, the victim." Vivian obviously found it hard to say the dead woman's name.

"That is a very good and troubling question," admitted Bonacourt.

"I'm afraid that's all I can tell you." Vivian pulled herself together and blew her nose noisily. Bonacourt watched her carefully. She'd be fine, she'd get over it, he thought, she was tough and resilient.

"Please stay within the building until further notice," he added, realizing that it was after three o'clock and nobody had had any lunch. As if on clue, Mallarmé appeared at the door with a proud look and delivered sandwiches.

"We all needed something to eat after the shock and all," he explained and handed both Bonacourt and Vivian a generous piece of baguette with brie and grapes on the side. Gratefully they accepted.

"You must have read our minds!" Bonacourt complimented him, which Mallarmé acknowledged by responding: "It wasn't so much your minds as our stomachs." Standing in the door, sandwich in hand Vivian turned around and suddenly said: "Now I know how Sarah felt. She had this guilty conscience about her father, as if it was her fault that he got into the fight with the priest, and she felt responsible for his death. Now I feel the same way about her death."

"Yes, but unlike Sarah, you'll be able to cope and get over it," Bonacourt answered without a trace of doubt in his voice. He asked Mallarmé to send in the tobacco storeowner.

Jean Bonnard stormed in full of indignation.

"Inspector, I have been waiting for three hours now, meanwhile my store remains closed, I haven't had any breakfast - or lunch - I am treated like a suspect and I don't even know what is going on!"

"Please have a seat and a sandwich Monsieur Bonnard," the inspector said pleasantly.

"You probably want to know my alibi for last night and all my movements from the moment your constable left until now!" said Jean, slightly deflated, and took the baguette.

"Sergeant," corrected the inspector mildly. "I also want to know if you have an alibi."

"As a matter of fact, and probably contrary to your expectations, I do!" Triumphantly, Jean took a bite out of his sandwich.

"That implies that you know the time of Madame Gluck's death."

"No, no that's not what I meant. Don't twist my words. I had a book club meeting at my house last night. We discussed *Crime and Punishment*, and I have eight witnesses!"

"Until when were they at your apartment?" asked Bonacourt.

"It must have been about eleven thirty. We talked and drank wine. We meet about once a month."

"Unfortunately that won't do any good. Madame Gluck died between two and three o'clock."

"Who has an alibi for two to three in the morning," asked Jean exasperated, his mouth full of brie.

"So what did you do at that time of night?" Bonacourt insisted.

"I slept, of course. Look, yesterday I was a suspect in Sarah Parker's murder, now I have to provide an alibi for the time Madame Gluck was killed. What am I? The local serial killer?"

"You did lie to us, monsieur."

"I did not lie. Maybe I withheld information. Only because I have been through this before many times, believe me it's not pleasant."

"You have been through a murder investigation?" Bonacourt asked doubtfully.

"I can't even think straight, and I can't even talk straight anymore. Of course I haven't been through a murder investigation, except after the accident happened. But I have experienced the suspicion before, this prejudice that just because twenty years ago a very tragic accident happened that took the life of an innocent person, a young girl actually, that because of that, for the rest of my life, I'll be a suspect for any crime in the neighborhood. I have paid dearly for my mistake. One moment of blinding sunlight, which prevented me from seeing the oncoming bicycle, followed by a lifetime of remorse. It is not in my nature to voluntarily hurt any living thing. It pains me more than anything to see people suffering. I had no interest in hurting Sarah. I liked her. I liked her very much. I could tell she was suffering. I wanted to help her, be her friend, not kill her. It's preposterous." Jean sank into his seat after this passionate speech.

Bonacourt regarded him neutrally. "Maybe she spurned your offers of friendship?" he suggested evenly. "If it is any consolation, you are not at the top of our suspect list. We are asking everybody for their alibi."

"She did not spurn, she did not accept, she did not respond. Sarah Parker lived in her own private all consuming hell. That's why I could relate to her. But it was a one-way emotion. She did not reciprocate," he said sadly.

"About the man in the blue BMW…" Bonacourt prompted.

"Yes, everybody is talking about the phantom in blue. I told your constable that I only saw him from afar, across the plaza. Not close enough to warrant an attack on my life. So don't worry about me."

"Sergeant," said Bonacourt automatically, "Mallarmé is a sergeant. I agree, I think you are probably not in immediate danger. Nevertheless we will have officers observing the building and the plaza."

"Watching who comes and goes?" Bonnard asked. "By the way, how would I have gotten into the building #13? I don't have a key, in contrast to many, who do!"

"I know," concluded Bonacourt.

Monday, May 25, D35 between Klingenthal - Strasbourg, 8:30 AM:

"What are you going to do today, Mommy?" asked Stevie from the backseat of the car on the way to school.

"I don't know yet, sweetheart."

"Grownups are so lucky," Daniel said bitterly from the passenger seat next to her. "They can do whatever they want! They can go to bed whenever they want, they can watch any movie they like—"

"Even R rated movies," Stevie interjected from the back.

"We on the other hand, have to go to school," Daniel continued, "and there we have to do what the teachers say, and when we come home we have to do what you tell us!" He ended his litany with a sigh.

"At least you can tell Mona what to do!" retorted Vega with a smile.

"But she doesn't even listen!" Stevie exclaimed in exasperation.

"Sometimes you guys don't listen to me either," considered Vega.

"But we can't tell you what to do!" Daniel said undeterred.

"You do try hard every day!" Vega replied.

"Don't you have to go to Mont Sainte Odile anymore?" Stevie asked.

"I don't have to go there, but I could," Vega admitted.

"See what I mean?" Daniel turned around to Stevie, who nodded vigorously. "She doesn't have to, but she can if she likes to! I'd like to have a choice like that about going to school!"

"Ah, you guys don't have it so bad. Plus you love school. And maybe I actually will go to Mont Sainte Odile today. Thanks for the suggestion." Both boys moaned in frustration.

Vega took the right turn in front of the convent gates and walked straight to the Spring of Tears. The path was soft, fragrant and shady, now that the May sunshine had dried the slippery, wet leaves of early spring and she encountered two hikers on her way. At the platform in front of the spring she sat down on a moss-covered stone and listened to the water gurgling soothingly from the rock. It was the only sound to be heard, and the peace and stillness of the forest permeated Vega's thoughts. "It is so hard to slow down to the pace to where it is possible to explore the mind," she remembered the abstract artist Agnes Martin saying. Maybe she could concentrate and think through the implications connected with the murders here at this quiet spot, where it had all begun.

It was hard to believe that this miraculous spring had been the location of a brutal mutilation and murder. She thought back to the day she had found Sarah's shoe and how it had changed her life. Since then she had abandoned her freelance writing project; had started exploring the dead woman's life; had gotten involved in the investigation; had met Inspector Bonacourt, Karl, the victim's brother, Jean, the tobacco store owner, and Mme. Gluck, now deceased. These people seemed to be part of her life now. She cared about them and was quite shaken by the news of the landlady's murder, which she had read in the newspaper this morning. Even though her encounter with the owner of the pension at Number 13 Place du Temple Neuf had been brief and not entirely pleasant, Vega felt that their lives had touched, however briefly, and that Mme. Gluck's death was connected to all the other events that had been set into motion since her discovery of the pink sling back. Vega tried to trace back the sequence of causes and effects. One incident had led to the next and this latest murder seemed to be the culmination. Could it have been avoided, Vega asked herself, or would it lead them closer to the killer? She had called the precinct and spoken briefly to Bonacourt, who was understandably busy. He had mentioned the strange arrangement of the body in the pose of Daumier's *Rue Transnonain,* a detail the newspaper had omitted, because of her background as an art historian. In the quiet of the beech forest, she summoned it in her mind: The corpse of an old man, with bare lags, exposed in his death: an innocent victim to a government revenge action for a sniper's gunshot from the victim's apartment building. The civil guards stormed the building and uniformly punished all its inhabitants by killing them in their sleep. This was in Paris in 1834. The killer of Mont Ste Odile knew about art, and maybe he also took revenge. Maybe Mme. Gluck was also an uninvolved bystander who had gotten in his way. But revenge for what?

Vega thought about Sarah being dragged here in the early morning hours to this remote and inconvenient spot. The killer cut out her eyes in an evil reversal of the miracle, which had restored Odile's sight, and then left Sarah behind the Spring of Tears. The pink shoe was positioned like an arrow toward the dead body. Vega realized that none of this was accidental. The killer had known exactly what he wanted to do. He had put up with the inconvenience of bringing his victim to this remote location so he could make a symbolic statement: Ste Odile gained her eyesight here; Sarah lost hers. The famous saint had begun to see, Sarah would never see again. Was she punished for seeing too much? It all tied together; the ancient pagan eye-water goddess had received her sacrifices here. Was Sarah the latest one? What had she seen, and what was she prevented from ever seeing again?

The spring inside its rocky niche behind the iron bars continued to murmur harmlessly. The forest smelled fresh and pungent. Vega tried to trace back the events from this particular spot in time to the initial cause that had led to Sarah's death here. For Sarah, the Spring of Tears had been the last stop of a journey that started many years ago; it was the culmination of an original trigger that eventually led to a disastrous effect. When had this sequence been initiated and set into motion? The lives of Sarah and her family had been knocked off course and forever altered by the encounter between her father and their parish priest. Vega was sure that the solution lay in this incident. Sarah's father had confronted the priest about something that so enraged him that he attacked the priest and almost killed him. What had the priest done to him or his family? Sarah had been thirteen or fourteen at the time. Judging from Sarah's letters, Vega assumed that he had tried to sexually abuse her. Had she told her father, who then challenged the pedophile? This had been in the 1960s when it was not easy to prove against the church an allegation of child molestation. Any official complaint probably would have been ignored and not have led anywhere. But if this was indeed the reason for the violent encounter, Sarah's father had hurt himself and his family more than the priest. In addition, the priest could not take revenge for the attack, because he was paralyzed and his assailant was dead anyway. However, it could account for Sarah's guilty conscience, because she was the one who had initiated the fatal visit that eventually destroyed her family, her father and ultimately herself.

Who was acting on behalf of the priest, and to what purpose? After thirty years, what was there to fear? Sarah would not have been able to press charges, discredit the priest or prove that he had abused her such a long time ago. The Stature of Limitations had long expired. What would she have gained? And why did her killer chase her all this time, trying to intimidate her, trying to prevent her from doing or exposing what? Why did he finally blind her to keep her from ever *seeing* again?

A gentle breeze caressed the canopy of foliage above her and created a small opening through which a few rays of the sun managed to break through and create a small column of light in the dark green background of the forest. Sarah had told Gary that Nazis were chasing her and that she possessed proof of their crime. The photo of the two blond young men, arm in arm, smiling at the camera appeared in her mind. Nazis plus crime plus art equaled what? All of a sudden, it became completely clear to Vega what she had to do.

Monday, May 25, Hagenau, 9:00 AM:

One of life's inexplicable patterns seems to be that times of great peacefulness and serenity are usually followed by utter chaos and mayhem. After the leisurely pace of the weekend the prefecture at Hagenau resembled a madhouse on Monday morning. It was a small police department in a small town, but everybody on staff was on duty. Bonacourt sat with his meager team in the small "incident" room. Actually, they had taken over the small meeting room, where the coffee machine stood and turned it into their headquarters. Pictures of the victim were taped to the wall. Bonacourt, Mallarmé, and Constable Vollard sat around the round table, which was cluttered with reports, and sipped their *café au lait*, taking the occasional bite from the fresh croissants Bonacourt had provided.

"Mallarmé, did you find the photograph Vivian Vetter spoke about listed in the inventory of Sarah Parker's belongings?"

"No, sir. It was not listed as one of the items found in her possession. There were only two photographs: one of Sarah with her father and one of her brother Karl with his little daughter, Rachel."

"That means the killer either found the picture when he searched Sarah's room or it is now in the possession of her brother Karl. I will follow up with Karl Parker. We all might have overlooked the picture."

"The picture seems to have been incriminating to the phantom. If he were indeed after the picture, and had already found it, then why would he go back and kill Madame Gluck,?" asked Marie Vollard.

"Because she had seen him. Behind sunglasses but still close up. Vega Stern had seen a picture of Sarah with sunglasses in a magazine, and she still recognized her. The phantom did not want to take a chance," Bonacourt explained patiently.

"Why did he go into the pension and expose himself in the first place?" asked Mallarmé.

"He needed to know the layout of the place, and Sarah's room number. He had to go in before he could search her room. Which brings us back to the crime at hand." Bonacourt reestablished his authority.

"Any results from the interviews with the other guests at the boarding house? Mallarmé, did anybody hear anything during the night of the murder?"

"No, sir. More precisely, they all said they did not hear anything unusual. There are always noises, they claim. People come and go, there is traffic in the plaza outside, people have their televisions on."

"At two in the morning?" Bonacourt followed up.

"I suppose not, but nobody remembers waking up at two o'clock."

"How could the phantom keep Madame Gluck so quiet when he stabbed her? She was a vocal woman and would have screamed and fought," considered Bonacourt.

"Chloroform!" explained Vollard. She had the forensics and pathology report in front of her. "The autopsy found traces of it. I am surprised we did not smell it on the scene."

"So the murderer smothered her with a strong anesthetic in her sleep and then stabbed her?" asked Bonacourt.

"So it seems. The report confirms three stab wounds, well placed into the heart. The killer knew what he was doing. It was not an impulsive act.

There is no evidence of rage, just the necessary stabs to the heart, and then the deliberate arrangement in the pose next to the bed," Vollard summed up.

"What about the neighbors? Did anybody living around the Place du Temple Neuf see or hear anything? There must be dozens of people, whose windows look out onto the plaza. Nobody had insomnia and looked out of the window, or heard a car drive up?" Bonacourt was grasping for straws.

Mallarmé was in charge of interrogations.

"As you say, there are a few dozen apartments and houses, and exactly two hundred twelve people to track down and interview. Strasbourg headquarters is handling the interviews. It will be a while before we hear anything."

Bonacourt knew it would be difficult to get much cooperation from the Strasbourg precinct. Under the leadership of Detective Garand they ran their own investigation, and even though the connection between Sarah Parker and Mme. Gluck's death seemed obvious to Bonacourt, Garand's department felt possessive of it, and would not give them immediate access to information they gathered.

"It was a Saturday night, and people tend to stay out late, and maybe have a drink or two. So if they hear a noise, it's not that unusual. They sleep deeper after a few glasses of wine," considered Mallarmé, who had not been out drinking in years.

"Well, we have to follow up the best we can. Mallarmé you are in charge of interviews. Vollard you stay in contact with forensics in regard to fingerprints or other traces. Did you speak to the travel agent? Did they refer any client from Germany driving a blue BMW to Sarah? Did they ever give her address to anybody?"

"The travel agency gave me their list of tourists and the dates when Sarah toured them through Strasbourg. But we don't know who to look for.

It is possible that the name of the suspect is on the list; it is also possible he gave a wrong name. They never give out addresses or contact information of guides to clients, but they admit it is possible that one of the clients followed Sarah home," Vollard reported.

"So that does not help us very much," concluded Bonacourt. "Do we have any connection with the Catholic diocese?"

"Bertrand from forensics is Catholic," volunteered Vollard.

"Good. Ask him to see if he can find out about the present location of Father Emanuel from the Parker's home parish church." Vollard made another notation in her notebook. "It seems like a long shot," Bonacourt continued, 'but we cannot afford to leave any stone unturned. I will interface with Detective Garand, and I'll speak to Karl Parker regarding the photo. We will stay in communication, of course. Anything else?"

"Yes, sir. What about the painting?" asked Mallarmé.

"I frankly don't know what to make of the arrangement of the body according to the Daumier print. I talked to Vega Stern. She is an art historian. Maybe she can help us with that."

"Sir, you'll need a translator in Germany for Karl Parker. Maybe she would agree to do that, and then you could talk to her about the Daumier," suggested Vollard.

"That's a possibility," admitted Bonacourt, thinking about Garand's reaction if he heard about such an unprofessional procedure.

"And what about that tobacco store guy, Jean Bonnard?" insisted Mallarmé. "He knows all about art, I told you. Did you mention it to him when you interviewed him?"

"In my estimation, I don't think he is capable of killing either one of the two victims," said Bonacourt.

"But he already killed before!" Mallarmé was not convinced.

"It would not hurt to question him again, Morris. Why don't you talk to him and mention the name *Daumier*, see if it means anything to him, if you get a reaction."

"How do you spell *Daumier*, inspector?" Mallarmé had his notebook ready.

Monday, May 25, Strasbourg, 10:30 AM:

After entering the Neoclassical library building, Vega passed images of Gutenberg on every floor, because Strasbourg can almost claim him as a son of the city. Vega tipped an imaginary hat to a sculpture of his likeness. The heels of her black and white sling-back shoes clicked loudly on the white marble floors. Coming into the dimness of the building from the exuberant May sunshine outside, helped her collect her thoughts and find her orientation. She steered toward the art section of the library and asked the young librarian for a catalogue entitled *Degenerate Art: The Fate of the Avant-Garde in Nazi Germany.*

"This is a reference catalogue only," the librarian said, as she handed the large hardback book with the rust-brown and sepia cover to Vega. "We have only one copy and we cannot allow it to leave the building."

"I understand. I am just so glad that the Los Angeles County Museum of Art re-created the exhibition and documented it in this catalogue. I refer to it all the time."

"It was really a showcase of avant-garde art," the librarian agreed. "Can you imagine artists like Picasso, van Gogh, Chagall, and Klee exhibited and held up for ridicule?" She shook her head in disbelief.

"Well, I think that was the intention, but most visitors who saw the *Degenerate Art* exhibit in 1937 knew that they were in the presence of great masters, and came to pay homage to them," Vega said, the heavy book in her arms now.

"And they came to say good-bye, because they knew that during the Nazi regime they were not going to see this kind of art again," continued the librarian, who obviously had a personal interest in the matter.

"Many of the paintings disappeared after the exhibit," Vega agreed. "They were either destroyed or sold or simply lost. Luckily the curators at LACMA managed to re-assemble some of the original paintings for their re-staging of the Degenerate Art exhibit in 1991."

"I wish I could have seen that show!" the librarian exclaimed wistfully.

"It was an unforgettable experience," admitted Vega, thinking about walking through the galleries with an increasing sense of horror at what the German people had done to the best artists of their generation and to the collectors, who had owned them. She knew very well that many paintings from the original exhibition were still missing and that just a small fraction had been reassembled.

"You saw it?" The librarian was envious.

A short line of people had accumulated behind Vega and they started to make subtle noises such as clearing their throats and shifting from leg to leg. Vega turned around with an apology, and the librarian nodded at her with an enthusiastic smile, as Vega carried her heavy load over to the nearest reading table. She laid out the digital image of the two brothers in front of her and then opened the big volume. In the beginning it showed photographs of the original exhibition mounted by the Nazi's *Reichskulturkammer* (Chamber of Culture) in Berlin. The galleries were crowded with people, slogans and paintings covering the walls in rows of two and three. The slogans, written directly onto the free wall space in a form of graffiti, mocked the art and the artists with anti-Jewish, anti-Communist propaganda such as: *Verhöhnung der deutschen Frau* ("An insult to German womanhood") under a wall of nudes, or *Bewusste Wehrsabotage* ("Deliberate sabotage of national defense") as a caption for paintings by Ernst Ludwig Kirchner and George Grosz. Vega moved through these pages quickly. She had seen them before.

The center of the catalogue consisted of an inventory of artists in alphabetical order, each with a biography and a list of works represented in the original 1937 exhibition. Out of around 16.000 modernist artworks confiscated by the Nazis from national museums and galleries, 650 were included. Some artists such as Wassily Kandinsky, Ernst Ludwig Kirchner, or Emil Nolde had ten or more paintings in the exhibition. Others had just one or two. Vega turned the pages until she arrived at the section devoted to Paul Klee, the Swiss artist, who had taught alongside Wassily Kandinsky at the groundbreaking Bauhaus School closed by the Nazi regime in 1933. Seventeen works by Klee were represented in the *Entartete Kunst* exhibit. Vega looked carefully at each of the ten reproductions in the catalogue and compared them with the picture behind the two brothers in the photograph. The childlike blocks of the painting with a bright circle of the moon floating above them reminded her strongly of Paul Klee's painting style. Klee believed in the "devotion to small things" (*Andacht zum Kleinen*) and usually used small format canvases. He wanted to "observe what goes unnoticed by the multitudes" and believed that mostly "children, lunatics, and primitives" have access to the magical realm of creation. He wanted to access this realm, and his work had a whimsical and childlike quality reminiscent of something out of a dream. One of the paintings in the catalogue, entitled *Wohin?* ("Where to?") from 1920 looked quite similar to the brothers' backdrop, but it did not include the moon. Nevertheless, Vega was convinced that she was on the right track, the painting in the photo was by Paul Klee. She scanned the list of Klee's works in the exhibition catalogue, and was struck by the entry *Mond über der Stadt* ("Moon above the city") from 1922. The entry read:

Painting, medium unknown, 39.5 x 52.2 cm. Acquired in 1923 by the Nationalgalerie, Berlin,

Room G2, NS inventory no. 16213; On Commission to Buchholz, sold 1939, location unknown;

Vega returned the book to the reference librarian and asked for Paul Klee's catalogue raisonné, the reference book that includes all the work ever created by a specific artist.

The librarian glanced up from her computer in surprise: "There are eight volumes. Paul Klee must have been a very prolific artist. We have only Volume III, about the years from 1919 to 22. Would you like to see that?"

Vega looked at her notes and nodded. *Moon of the City* was dated 1922. It took the librarian a while to fetch the heavy volume and when she finally heaved it across the counter Vega felt her heart sinking. How was she possibly going to find a painting for which she just had a vague black and white partial image and a hunch that it could be from Paul Klee? At the table she leafed through pages and pages of gorgeous and whimsical drawings, and paintings all created in the short span of three years. "The artist Paul Klee had an overwhelming desire to create", she thought. Together with Kandinsky, his colleague at the Bauhaus School for Art and Design in Weimar, Dessau and Berlin, he had been declared a degenerate artist. After the Nazis closed the school, Klee and Kandinsky were out of a job and feared for their safety. Kandinsky fled to France, as the return to his native Russia was barred by the reign of Communism there. Klee returned to his native Switzerland, where he continued to paint until his death in 1940. Vega thought about their own Klee etching, which hung in their large living room. Greg had found it in a small gallery on one of his business trips in Geneva. It had been created in 1939, the year before Klee's death in his native town Bern, Switzerland. Therefore they knew, the etching's provenance was beyond suspicion.

Vega approached the entry for 1922 and under number 2842 found a small black and white image of *Mond über der Stadt*. She scanned the description and provenance and it confirmed that the location of the painting was unknown. Her heart beat faster and she pulled out her photo of the brothers to compare the painting in the background with the small reproduction in front of her. Unfortunately it was not a match. Vega felt disappointed, but then she realized that all the paintings in the Degenerate Art Exhibition had been confiscated from museums, this particular one from the Nationalgalerie in Berlin. If her hunch was correct, the picture she was looking for had been taken from the home of a private collector.

Vega was not sure what to do next. She returned the book to the librarian.

"Is there any reference work about artwork stolen in Germany during the Nazi era?" she asked hopefully.

"There are a few good websites," the librarian replied. "You can try *www.lostart.de*. They list art that is still missing. You can use one of our computers if you like." She pointed to a row of computers with Internet access.

Vega sat down and accessed the German website established to list lost and found art, trying to match up former owners or their heirs with artwork plundered or stolen during the Nazi regime. She typed in the name *Paul Klee* as a search option, and twenty-three objects popped up. Going down the list, she realized only one was accompanied by an image, and it was not the picture she was looking for. About half of the missing Paul Klee paintings and prints listed had been confiscated in the year 1937 as "degenerate art" and retained by the Ministry of Propaganda and People's Education at a storage facility in Güstrow. At the end of WWII, in 1945, the Red Army cleaned out the entire art inventory and most likely Russian soldiers or government officials, took these works back home as war bounty.

Vega was surprised that *Moon over the City* was not among those paintings listed. Eight works by Klee had been taken from a collector named John Anthony Thwaites. A few works did not describe the former owners or circumstances of their loss, and one painting, entitled *Dammweg/Waldsteg* ("Forest Trail") from 1929 had been part of the Max Silberberg collection and had been confiscated in 1939 in Breslau. Vega's heart made a little jump as she remembered Karl telling her that his father fled from the Red Army and the Russian occupation in Breslau to southern Germany. Unfortunately the website did not provide an image for *Dammweg/Waldsteg*. She had a feeling it might look like the painting in the background of the photo in front of her. Following an intuition she typed in the name *Daumier*, thinking of the strange arrangement of Mme. Gluck's corpse. Thirty-three objects by Daumier were listed in the database and when Vega scrolled down and checked their provenance, the Silberberg collection in Breslau promptly came up again. A Daumier drawing, entitled *Seinelandschaft/Fluss mit Brücke* (Seine landscape with bridge) was confiscated in Breslau in 1939 from the Silberberg collection, just as the Klee painting had been.

"Bingo!" she said to herself and the serious scholar at the computer next to her looked at her with raised eyebrows.

Vega went back to her search engine and typed in *Max Silberberg* and the database spit out a list of twenty-three missing artworks from the Silberberg collection, including paintings by Gustav Klimt, Paul Signac, Alexei Jawlensky, Paul Klee, and Honoré Daumier, as well as some lesser known artists. Vega pictured this carefully assembled collection somewhere in a graceful villa in Breslau decorating the walls and hallways. Then one day in 1939 a Nazi commando stormed in and confiscated the whole lot. Did it happen unexpectedly? What had happened to the owners? Did they have warning? Could they save some of their work and could they save themselves?

Vega took notes of everything she had found out so far and then closed up the *Lostart* website and went to the Google search engine instead. She typed in Max Silberberg's name and hit enter. A short biography from the National Gallery in Washington came up:

Max Silberberg, Polish, died c. 1944

Max Silberberg was a wealthy industrialist in Breslau, Germany (now Wroclaw, Poland). He began collecting art, primarily Impressionist paintings, in the 1920s. After the Nazis came to power in 1933, Silberberg, who was Jewish, was forced out of his job. His art collection of over 143 paintings was sold at four forced auctions in Berlin between 1933 and 1938. Silberberg's son Alfred and daughter-in-law Gerta fled to Britain just prior to the war, but Silberberg and his wife remained in Germany, where they are assumed to have died in a concentration camp. Two pictures from the Silberberg collection are now in the National Gallery of Art, having been purchased in Paris in 1932 by Chester Dale.

The paragraph answered Vega's questions. Max Silberberg had not been able to save himself, his wife, or his collection. At least his son Alfred had escaped the Nazis to Britain. How anybody could enjoy owning art obtained in such a manner was beyond Vega's comprehension. It must be like staring your crime right in the eye every time you looked at the stolen pictures. Maybe that was part of what had driven the thief to pursue Sarah and the only proof of his theft so relentlessly. Vega wondered if Karl could confirm whether his father had had a friend named Alfred Silberberg and whether he had seen Alfred's father's collection during visits to his house. Alfred and Sarah's father would have been the same age. Seeing the same painting in a photograph behind the smiling priest, knowing full well what had happened to the picture and his owner, might have driven Sarah's father to the irrational act of attacking the priest.

Vega looked up from the computer screen. It was time for her to call Bonacourt and to pick up her children. She thanked the librarian and asked her if she could possibly order the fifth Volume of the Paul Klee catalogue raisonné, which would include the 1929 picture *Dammweg/Waldsteg* and could prove what so far was based only on circumstantial evidence and a very strong hunch. The librarian promised to try to order it from the Paul Klee Foundation in Switzerland, but it could take a while. She would call Vega and let her know when it arrived.

Vega stepped out of the cool, quiet, and shady library into the blinding sunlight. She stood on the entrance steps of the library and dialed Bonacourt's number on her cell phone.

He answered immediately.

"Ah, Madame Stern, I have been trying to reach you. Your cell phone did not pick up."

"Inspector, I was in the library, I had to turn it off. I think I have some new and interesting information for you."

"So do I, madame. Are you ready to go to a nursing home in Germany?"

"Nursing homes are not exactly my favorite places to go, but if you think it is important… When do we go?"

"How about I pick you up in an hour?"

"Make that an hour and a half. I have to pick up the boys and make sure they are taken care of."

"Very well. We'll meet you at your house in ninety minutes."

He hung up, and Vega scrambled down the stairs and to her car wondering what important developments had taken place while she had been buried in the library.

Monday, May 25, Klingenthal, 3:30 PM:

"Mom, why are we racing home like this?" Stevie asked from the backseat as Vega navigated the curves between Strasbourg and Klingenthal with screeching tires.

"Because I have to go to Germany with the inspector. He is picking me up shortly and I have to make sure you guys are taken care of."

"Are you going to visit Grandma in Germany?"

"No, we are going to a nursing home."

"That's where Grandma lives."

"There are many different nursing homes, sweetheart. This one has to do with the dead girl."

"Sarah Parker," nodded Daniel from the passenger seat. "Did you find something out about her?"

"I think so. I did some research in the library today."

"I do research all the time in my school library," Stevie said. "I found out so much information about mercury the other day. Did you know that it is the name of a planet, a metal, and a god?"

"Stevie, you are always full of unusual information," said Vega.

Daniel snorted contemptuously. "How could you find anything in the library about a murder victim?" he insisted.

"I found out about a painting by a famous artist that was stolen fifty years ago and was never given back."

"I should have known it would be something about paintings and art!" sighed Daniel. "But are you going to catch the killer?"

"I think we still have a ways to go before we find him. But maybe we are getting closer."

"You sound like a real detective, Mom. I think being a detective is much cooler than writing articles about Mont Ste Odile," Stevie asserted.

"Yes, but that's where it all started!" Vega concluded.

They had reached the house and saw the inspector's car already waiting. Fortunately Greg was home and took the kids so that Vega could climb directly into the backseat of the unmarked Renault, where Bonacourt was waiting and Mallarmé sat behind the wheel. They took off and Vega told Bonacourt about her research and the missing paintings from the Silberberg collection. When she showed him the photo of the two smiling men in front of what she suspected was one of them, he whistled.

"Madame, we have been looking for this photo! Sarah Parker's neighbor Vivian Vetter told us about the importance of a photograph Sarah possessed and that whoever pursued her, wanted to get hold of this picture. It is one of the reasons we are driving to Germany today! You should have shared this information with us a lot earlier!"

Vega blushed.

"I couldn't—I mean—I wasn't really supposed to look through her things, but I couldn't help it, and after I found it something struck me about the painting in the background. I suddenly thought, 'It is not the foreground and the people that are important, it's the painting in the background.' And even though it was black and white and partially obstructed it looked like a Paul Klee to me. It just suddenly clicked in my mind that the photo was the proof the killer was after. It showed him in front of a painting that he should not possess. A painting that was acquired under criminal circumstances from a collector that ended up in a concentration camp."

"Well, I am glad that it was you who found the picture and not the phantom, but nevertheless, if we had had this picture earlier, we might have been able to prevent the second murder," Bonacourt said gravely.

Vega sat thunderstruck. She had not considered that possibility, being too caught up in her recent discoveries. "Oh my god", she thought, "now I am going to join the club of the guilty, like Vivian, and Sarah, who had to live with the knowledge that because of their actions a person might have died."

The inspector was not about to ease her mind.

"Besides, the people in the photo are important as well. If we are correct in our assumption, they are Father Emanuel, aka Paul Prattler, and his brother, Fritz Prattler."

Now it was Vega's turn to whistle.

"You found the name of the phantom?" she exclaimed.

"We found the name of Sarah and Karl Parker's parish priest, who was attacked by their father in 1975. We also found the name of his brother. Whether he is the phantom and whether they are connected to the murders is at this point pure conjecture!" he cautioned.

"But the picture is the proof! He stole the painting, and it was most likely not the only one. I bet he stole a Daumier as well. Remember the arrangement of Madame Gluck's body in the form of the Daumier print? I checked Daumier's name and found out that Max Silberberg in Breslau had a Daumier painting called *Seine Landscape, River with Bridge*, which was stolen at the same time as the Klee, and it's also still missing!"

"Do you have a picture of the actual Paul Klee paintings that we could use to compare to the photo?"

" No, not yet. But I am working on it. We need to access the catalogue raisonné of the artist. I ordered one from the Paul Klee Foundation in Switzerland."

"In that case all we have is a hunch. If we had been able to show this photo to Madame Gluck, she could have told us whether it was indeed the same person who came and inquired about Sarah before her death. But it is too late for that now."

Vega knew, of course, that Bonacourt was right. On the other hand, it occurred to her that the police should have found the picture themselves when they examined Sarah's belongings. Why hadn't they been as thorough as she? It made her feel a little better, but she decided not to bring up this point right now. She might have to use it later, if the accusations continued.

"We could show it to Jean Bonnard," Mallarmé interjected from the driver's seat. The tobacco storeowner still seemed to be on Mallarmé's mind.

"He only saw the phantom from afar, and the photo is probably thirty years old, but it could not hurt," Bonacourt admitted. "Did you talk to him about Daumier?"

Mallarmé shifted in his seat uncomfortably and reported over his shoulder: "I mentioned the name to him and asked him if it meant something to him. He launched into a lecture about Daumier and how important he was for the rise of realism in art and his courage in regard to social criticism. Then he told me that artists nowadays don't care about social issues anymore, even though we still have a class system, just like in Daumier's time, and that justice is not blind, but favors those with money. He gave me an earful, certainly a lot more than I ever wanted to know. He is a real socialist, I tell you, we should keep an eye on him!"

Bonacourt smiled. "Nothing of value then?" he asked.

"He seemed a little too forthcoming about the subject to hide a guilty conscience," Mallarmé admitted. "Then he asked me why I wanted to know, and I had to make up something. I probably wasn't too convincing."

"The Daumier connection Madame Stern came up with seems a little bit more promising," concluded Bonacourt.

Vega nodded. She looked out the window at the dense dark pine trees of the Black Forest gliding by. She had to think of the proverb: *Den Wald vor lauter Bäumen nicht sehen* ("Not seeing the forest for all the trees"). It was right in front of them, but they could not see it.

"How did you find the name of the priest?" she asked.

"It was not too difficult for our computer wiz at the station to get access to the records of the diocese and look up the year and the Parker home parish. Their priest was Paul Prattler. We finally realized he was the key. The diocese gave us the name of the nursing home where he was transferred after the injury. Karl will meet us there. I had asked him to look for the photo again. Now that won't be necessary, as we already have it. We will verify if Paul Prattler is indeed the young priest in the picture and if the other person is his brother. Then we will try to find out what really happened during that fateful encounter between him and Sarah Parker's father. I think your research will be helpful. Paul Prattler may not even know about the significance of the painting in the background."

Vega said nothing. She thought it was unlikely that Prattler was an innocent bystander in the art theft and the ensuing years of pursuit of Sarah Parker. She still wanted to know why Sarah's father went to confront the priest in the first place, before discovering this photo on Paul's desk.

A black Mercedes drove up dangerously close behind them and blinded them with his high beams annoyingly. Mallarmé cursed under his breath and pulled out of the fast lane to the right. "Mercedes drivers think they have built in right-of-way. Arrogant bastards!" he muttered.

"Where would an art thief go with valuable and recognizable paintings?" Vega asked nobody in particular.

"It would have been difficult to get them out of the country in the 1950s. He may have hidden them within Germany," guessed Bonacourt.

"He could not sell them, at least not at auction or through a gallery," Vega continued, "Those places have access to the *Lostart* websites and they are getting more aware about provenance issues by the year."

"If there is no image of the stolen work on the website, as you say, it would be hard to identify." Bonacourt considered.

"True. However, if an authentic, but as yet not accounted for, Klee or Daumier suddenly showed up, it would cause a bit of a stir in the art market," Vega said.

Their Renault approached the outskirts of Stuttgart. The forest outside the windows began to thin, and was slowly replaced by fields, meadows, shopping centers, and multi-story housing developments. It all looked very orderly but bland. Vega stared outside silently. She thought about Mme. Gluck and the chain of events that had led to her death. Could she have prevented her murder if she had shared the photo of the two brothers with the police sooner? She tried to trace back time to the moment when she had made the decision that led to the current state of affairs: She had been in the bedroom, looking through the box with Sarah's belongings. The scroll had intrigued her. Probably the decisive moment was when she turned around the *thangka* and examined its back. She had stumbled upon the photo, taken a digital image, and looked at it for a few moments. Then Stevie and Daniel had demanded their dinner and it had not even occurred to her to do anything other than return the photo to its hiding place. Reporting the discovery had really not even been a question in her mind, and at no point had she made a conscious decision to withhold this piece of evidence. Besides, the children had distracted her. However, she knew, she was guilty of searching through Sarah's belongings and that her reasoning and excuses would not be able to stand up to her conscience in the long run. She could have shown the digital image to the inspector at any time. Besides, failing to make a conscious, ethical decision did not absolve her from responsibility.

Vega noticed the gloomy, overcast sky outside. Nowhere here was any evidence of the exuberant, brilliant May day that had sparkled and glittered in Strasbourg only 100 km away. Whenever she entered Germany coming from France, the enormous change and difference struck and amazed Vega. Two countries situated side by side, with the Alsace switching nationalities back and forth several times over the past century, sitting right in the middle of them. The difference between the countries was so noticeable and obvious that even without a border station, you could not miss it. On the French side, the roads had slightly more potholes, the buildings were older, and the traffic was more chaotic, winding through traffic circles and side streets, marked by bistros and small flowerbeds in the middle. Whereas the German Autobahn was straight and efficient but clogged with trucks and lovingly polished luxury cars. Buildings along the road were square, gray, and orderly and without much decoration except for the obligatory geranium pots on the windowsills. Even the weather seemed to participate in the grayness and gloominess of the surroundings.

"I am being completely unfair and grossly generalizing," Vega thought to herself. "It's just because I am in such a bad mood and also because I am so enchanted with my new home in Klingenthal. I don't miss living in Germany and I don't have too many good memories about growing up here."

Vega thought about Sarah, who obviously had entertained similar feelings and preferred to live in a cheap pension in Strasbourg rather than in her home country. Considering all Vega knew about Sarah by now, her choice made perfect sense. Sarah's memories of Germany had been much worse than Vega's, but for both they extended back to before the time either of them had been born. They had to deal with the collective national guilt of being born German and belonging to a people that had been capable of the worst atrocities humankind was capable of imagining. It was a burden to be born as part of a race that had once hailed itself superior and most beautiful, only to reveal the ugliest soul underneath its blond and blue-eyed surface. Somehow this period of German history almost cancelled out Beethoven, Dürer, Goethe, and Friedrich Nietzsche. As a teenager Vega had always hated her blond hair and pale white skin, which identified her German origin wherever she went. If she had lived during the Nazi regime, she would have been embraced as a worthy member of the Aryan race. Instead, Vega wanted to look like the Italian actress Sophia Loren, whose pictures she had cut out of the women's magazine her mother read and taped them to the wall above her bed. She admired her dark and smoldering beauty, the large, chocolate brown eyes and the generous, curvaceous figure, which was in every way the opposite of her own tall and slim frame. She wondered if there was something like a collective, national Karma, a huge negative balance in Germany's moral bank account that had to be paid off by all its citizens for decades and generations to come, no matter if they had been alive during the Second World War or not. Did she have to continue carrying this guilt regardless how far she fled, whether it was to California or just across the border into France?

Vega shook herself out of her daydream, as she noticed that Mallarmé had exited the freeway and stopped at a red light. She knew this intersection well; it was the same exit she took in order to reach her mother's nursing home.

"Where exactly are we going?" she asked.

"It's a Catholic nursing home run by the diocese called St. Sophie," explained Mallarmé over his shoulder from the driver's seat. Bonacourt continued to read his files in preparation for their encounter with father Emanuel.

"My mother is in the same home!" Vega exclaimed, "I go there about once a week."

The inspector raised his eyebrows and mumbled "What a coincidence," as if he didn't believe in coincidences.

"Excellent," Mallarmé beamed at her happily. "Then you can give me directions how to get there. The ones I have are very confusing."

Vega told him to get in to the left lane, make a turn and then a second left, and mentally prepared herself, as always, for the encounter with her mother. She had not expected to see her today, but it was of course unavoidable, once they got to St. Sophie, where all the staff knew her. Her mother, Martha, had experienced Hitler's third Reich personally, in contrast to any member of Vega's generation. Born in 1931, Martha had been two when Hitler came to power. She had been nine when her school was firebombed and burned down to the ground, which at the time made Martha very happy. She hated school and all her half-crazy teachers, who had only been exempt from military duty because they were either mentally or physically disabled. Martha's math teacher, she had told Vega when she was still able to tell stories, used to jump underneath the table at each unexpected noise and remained there, shivering, until the school bell announced the end of the lesson. Less pleasant than the destruction of her hated school, was Martha's evacuation at age ten out of the city and into the country. Separated from her mother and siblings, she was placed with a farmer's family, who screened her letters, resented every scrap of food they gave her, and forced her to work long hours in the fields.

Vega was not sure whether it had been those experiences, the countless nights spent in bomb shelters listening to the explosions above, or the terrible years of hunger after the war that damaged her mother's soul. When Vega's grandfather finally returned home after four years in a Russian prisoner of war camp in Siberia, a stranger now to his wife and three children, he forbade them to laugh, beat them, and scolded them for their disrespect of all the suffering he had seen. Forty years later Vega's mother still awoke screaming from nightmares about fighter planes flying overhead and other horrors she had seen. She could or would not articulate what demons haunted her from a distant but not forgotten past. Asking her mother about them only made her angry and caused Martha to shut herself off. Now, she existed in a strange in-between state, beyond the space-time continuum most people shared. She was stuck in her own mind, in her own memory, without the words or the gestures to reach out and reconnect with the rest of humankind. Whenever Vega visited, she tried to share her mother's world with her for a while, and tried to imagine the ghosts that populated it, because she knew, Martha could not share and participate in Vega's world anymore.

They had reached the parking lot of the nursing home, and Mallarmé brought the Renault to a stop. Bonacourt collected his files and gave orders.

"Okay, we'll confront Paul Prattler with the photo and then I'll ask a few questions, which Madame Stern can translate."

"Yes sir," Mallarmé and Vega said in unison.

They met Karl Parker in the entrance lobby of the nursing home, which was furnished with comfortable wooden chairs and tables, interspersed with green plants and birdcages to give the place the feeling of a living room. Karl Parker sat awkwardly between an ancient inmate in a wheelchair and a birdcage full of chirping yellow canaries. He seemed relieved to see Bonacourt and his entourage approaching

"Inspector Bonacourt," he began urgently, "I did not find the photo."

"It's all right, Herr Parker," Bonacourt answered reassuringly, "Madame Stern has provided us with a copy!"

Karl shot Vega an icy and suspicious glance, but she just shrugged in response. They rode the elevator to the second floor, where the director met them and agreed to let them use his meeting room for the interview with Paul Prattler in the presence of Sister Margaret. The room turned out to be bright and pleasant with a window overlooking ripening wheat and cabbage fields. The kind-looking director, who had a neatly trimmed beard and sparkling eyes behind tortoiseshell glasses, shook their hands, welcomed Vega back, assured her that her mother was well, and promised his cooperation as long as it did not interfere with the well-being of his "guests", as he called the inhabitants of his institution. He retreated into his office next door, where they should join him after the interview. Sister Margaret sat plump and complacent, hands folded in her lap, in a wicker chair next to Paul Prattler's wheelchair. The sight of the old priest startled and chilled Vega. She had seen his withered face staring at her many times, when she came for her visits, with eyes as vicious and defiant, as they were small and sunken into his bony skull. His wrinkled neck snaked out of his starched priest's collar like that of an ancient turtle. His left hand lay limply in his lap, the wooden beads of his rosary loosely wrapped around the gnarled fingers. The right hand hung lifelessly on his side, just as the entire right side of his face and body seemed to sag away from the middle, paralyzed and useless. Vega noticed the small mole on his forehead.

"Father Emanuel, or should I call you Herr Prattler, I am Inspector Bonacourt and this is Sergeant Mallarmé and Madame Stern, who will translate a few questions," Began Bonacourt. "I trust you remember Herr Karl Parker, who was in your congregation 25 years ago, together with his sister Sarah and his mother." He paused and looked at Prattler for any reaction, but none was visible, except that his eyes sparkled angrily and darted back and forth between his visitors.

"You do remember, I am sure, Herr Friedrich Parker, Karl Parker's father, even though he wasn't part of your congregation, don't you?" prompted Bonacourt.

"Father Emanuel can barely speak," Sister Margaret interjected. "He understands, but his paralysis is so severe that he cannot really articulate any words."

Bonacourt looked utterly deflated.

"Can he nod?" he asked desperately.

"He can nod slightly, and he can scrawl a few words onto a writing pad with his left hand," Sister Margaret assured them.

"Do you remember Friedrich Parker and his children Sarah and Karl?" Bonacourt asked point blank. The priest nodded almost invisibly.

"Of course he remembers", thought Vega, "Friedrich Parker reduced him to the state he is in now."

Bonacourt continued.

"I know, these memories must be very painful for you, but Sarah Parker was murdered earlier this month and we have reason to believe that the cause of her death lies in the encounter you had with her father thirty years ago."

At the mention of Sarah Parker's death something resembling a smile arose on Paul Prattler's asymmetrical lips. He did not seem surprised or shocked by this piece of information.

"Why did Friedrich Parker come to see you in the first place?" Bonacourt asked, knowing full well that the old man could not answer him. "Had something been going on between you and Sarah Parker?" Bonacourt continued. Again the old man did not answer, but a little grimace resembling a smirk contorted his parched lips.

"Be that as it may," Bonacourt resumed and pulled out the photograph of the two smiling, young men and showed it to Prattler.

"Did Friedrich Parker remove this photograph from your desk during your encounter?"

This time Prattler's eyes betrayed his shock and surprise at the sight of the picture. He nodded very slightly.

"Is this a photograph of you and your brother?" Bonacourt quickly followed up. Again the old man nodded. "What about the painting in the background. Does it belong to your brother?"

This was a loaded question and the priest became very agitated. His head shook from side to side and his body twitched in the wheelchair. His left hand made grasping motions and Sister Margaret put a pen between his fingers and held a writing pad underneath. With painfully slow, scraggly letters the priest began to spell out:

GO TO HELL!

Reading this message left them momentarily speechless.

Sister Margaret recovered most quickly. "Now Father Emanuel that is really not a nice thing to say to your guests," she scolded, "You should be ashamed of yourself, being a priest and all! How could you wish something like that on anybody!"

The old man's hand twitched and again he started to scrawl letters onto the pad:

I AM IN HELL!

After Prattler had put the last shaky dot underneath his exclamation mark, muffled noises came out of his speechless throat and his body contorted in spasm. Sister Margaret tried to calm him down, declaring that of course he was not going to hell and that the good Lord forgave all of them for their sins, but she had a hard time restraining him.

"Did you threaten Sarah Parker?" Vega suddenly asked. "Did you tell her if she told anybody that you sexually abused her, she'd go to hell?"

The old priest's head swiveled around and his bloodshot eyes fixed themselves onto hers.

SHE BURNS IN HELL! he wrote in slow painful letters.

Sister Margaret had had enough. "What is all this talk about hell, Father Emanuel? You are not yourself today. You are not answering the questions these visitors are asking. Now, does this picture in the photograph belong to your brother? You can answer with a yes or no!"

Prattler nodded and then became so agitated that Sister Margaret could not restrain him and had to declare the interview as over.

Bonacourt and Mallarmé left the room to speak to the director. Bonacourt wanted to ask him if Prattler had contact with his brother, and Vega climbed one more set of stairs to the third floor and her mother's room. Because it was an overcast day, and because the time was short, she just sat holding her mother's small and almost weightless hand, singing to her softly the songs of her childhood. Silent tears rolled down her mother's sunken cheeks, as she listened and cried, not entirely unhappily.

Monday, May 25, Stuttgart, 6:45 PM:

As Vega descended to the lobby forty-five minutes later, she found Karl Parker talking agitatedly to Bonacourt:

"Gary told me what Father Emanuel did to Sarah, and I don't need to repeat the gory details, except that this guy is a real pig. Sarah finally told our dad, who understandably went to confront Father Emanuel in a considerable rage. While in Emanuel's office, he discovered the photo of the two brothers on Prattler's desk and recognized the painting in the background from his childhood friend Alfred Silberberg's house."

"That's how it seems," confirmed Bonacourt. "Did your father ever mention Alfred or his father Max Silberberg and their art collection?"

"Yes, I remember him talking about his childhood friend Alfred many times and how he loved going to their villa. Alfred's father, Max, was a very successful and kind man. He donated several of his artworks to the Schlesische Museum in Breslau, but of course, received no gratitude for it. My dad told me how the whole family just disappeared one day. His friend Alfred managed to get away to England. But Max and his wife ended up in a concentration camp." Karl paused. "During his visits to the villa, Max Silberberg sometimes talked to my dad about the paintings, because he noticed my dad's interest in art. Later my father took us to museums and he showed us paintings by the artists he had first seen at the Silberberg's villa: Paul Signac, the French impressionists, Paul Klee, Alexei Jawlensky, and Gustav Klimt, Daumier. He always said that Max Silberberg opened his eyes to modern art. Without Max Silberberg, he'd have never known about the beauty and power that colors and lines can have. He said, the least we could do in Max Silberberg's memory was to pay tribute to the artists he loved."

Karl stopped and they all stood silently for a moment, imagining this kind man, amidst his precious art collection that gave him so much pleasure and that he loved to share with others.

"If my dad indeed recognized a painting from the Max Silberberg collection in the background of a photo with a smiling Fritz and Paul Prattler, then I can fully understand his anger, because he knew what had happened to Max Silberberg and his collection!" Karl concluded.

"Fritz Prattler?" Vega asked.

Bonacourt nodded. "The director of the nursing home confirmed that Paul Prattler has a brother two years his junior, named Fritz. However, they haven't seen him in years. The Diocese pays for Prattler's stay, so the home has no official dealings with the brother, but his last address is listed as Paradies Strasse, not far from here. I don't think we'll find him there, but we must go by and check if somebody remembers him."

"Isn't it an extraordinary coincidence that Prattler, or his brother, had been in Breslau before the war like your father and that they then met again in Stuttgart?" asked the pragmatic Mallarmé.

"No, it's not a coincidence at all!" explained Karl. "My parents had a difficult time assimilating in the West and they gravitated toward other Silesian immigrants. My mother chose this congregation because its pastor was from her hometown."

"Not the best choice," Vega remarked. Karl nodded.

"Emanuel threatened Sarah if she ever told anybody about what he did to her, she'd burn in hell. And she lived in her own hell," Karl suddenly burst out.

"It became a self-fulfilling prophecy," Vega confirmed.

Karl had to return to Tübingen. He looked drained and exhausted, but he was also relieved by the knowledge that they were getting closer to his sister's murderer and the mystery that surrounded her death.

"I really hope you find this Fritz Prattler," he said, as he shook Vega's and Bonacourt's hands, "I blame him for the deaths of my father and my sister."

"Not to mention Madame Gluck and several priceless works of art," mumbled Mallarmé.

"Thank you for your help and effort," Karl added haltingly as he looked into Vega's eyes.

"You are very welcome."

Vega felt exhausted herself. It had been a very long day. Starting at the Spring of Tears, where she had the sudden revelation about the importance of the artwork, to the library and her emotionally draining findings about the disappearance of the Silberberg collection, to the jarring encounter with the old priest, who sat trapped in his wheelchair and his own mind, tortured by the demons he had summoned.

"I think I need something to eat before we go to Paradies Strasse," she said weakly. Bonacourt and Mallarmé smiled indulgently and stopped at an Imbiss close by, where they ate Curry Wurst and Pommes Frittes, standing around one of the high tables on the sidewalk.

"We are definitely not in France anymore," commented Mallarmé wistfully as he washed down a soggy bite of sausage with some Coke.

"I feel better, though," Vega reported, as she dipped her last French fry into a pile of oily mayonnaise.

"Let's go then," commanded Bonacourt, who was not eager to linger any longer over this less than civilized dining experience. They climbed back into the Renault and rode into the descending darkness. The gloomy, gray day turned into a gloomy, starless night.

Paradies Strasse was indeed only a short drive away and soon they rolled along a quiet, well-lit residential street. Stately two- and three-story homes behind well-tended gardens, with rosebushes that smelled fragrant in the night air, lined the left side of the street. The right side dropped off behind a border of trees and bushes into a canyon, where train tracks ran. Mallarmé parked the Renault in front of the house number the director had given to them. The handsome honey-colored building had three floors, a large terrace, a lush garden, and a brightly lit picture window on the first floor.

"At least someone is at home!" Bonacourt remarked as he checked his watch. It was 7:30 pm, early enough to ring the bell of this respectable home. An elderly woman with a strong Swabian accent opened the door, and after she saw Bonacourt's police ID, ushered them in with a barrage of welcoming and encouraging remarks. They joined her and her husband in deep, old-fashioned leather chairs in front of the picture window.

"They are looking for Herr Prattler, Egon," she explained to her husband, who nodded knowingly. "Herr Prattler used to rent the ground floor from us," she added helpfully, "But he left, well it must have been five years ago. Yes, it was before we went on our trip to China, five and a half years ago." She nodded, happy to be able to pin-point Prattlers time of departure. "We decided not to rent the apartment out anymore. You never know who you get. My husband and I are getting older and we don't want strangers in the house anymore. You know how it is in this country, if you get a bad tenant, there is nothing you can do to get him out. All the laws protect the renters, not the landlords. We now keep the apartment for our daughter and son. When they come to visit they can stay there and have their own space. It works out better for everybody, right Egon?"

"Was Herr Prattler a bad tenant?" Bonacourt gently interrupted the flow.

"Well no, I could not say he was bad. He was always polite, and he paid his rent on time, but we did not quite feel comfortable with him, did we Egon?" Again Egon nodded wisely.

"Why didn't you feel comfortable with him?" Mallarmé asked the follow-up question.

"He was so secretive and almost standoffish, right Egon? Don't you remember the time when I just went downstairs to bring him a jar of my homemade raspberry jam? I make very good raspberry jam, with lemon and only real fruit and sugar, no preservatives. People love my jam, so I thought I'll bring him a jar. He's a bachelor and he probably does not get a lot of homemade food. He never seemed to cook, while he lived here, always went out to eat, even though the apartment has a very nice kitchen. So, I rang his doorbell and he didn't answer. Then I called, because I knew he was home, his car was right outside. I said, 'Herr Prattler, I brought you some home made raspberry jam; I'll leave it right in front of your door.' He suddenly opens the door and he was really upset. He stands there in the hallway, barely 10 centimeters away from me, and he closes the door behind him as if I was going to spy what's inside, and he says to me in a really cold kind of voice, 'Don't do this anymore! Don't come to my apartment unannounced! I don't appreciate it and I don't eat jelly'. Remember that, Egon? Now, you must know, inspector, that I am not a person who is easily intimidated, even though he was about a foot and a half taller than me and he talked down to me rather threateningly. But I said, 'You don't have to threaten me; I just wanted to give you a gift.' And he grumbled something of an apology and went back inside his apartment."

"How long did he live here?" Mallarmé asked.

"Oh, just over a year, wasn't it, Egon? He had no friends, no visitors; frankly, I was glad to see him go."

"Do you know where he moved?" Bonacourt asked.

"Oh no, he just suddenly gave notice; he did not volunteer a reason or a forwarding address, and frankly, I did not ask."

"What about his mail? Didn't he receive the occasional piece of mail after leaving that had to be forwarded?" Mallarmé asked.

"He did not receive mail here. He had a post office box."

Vega had been looking around the comfortable living room; thick Persian carpets, the mahogany sideboard with glass doors full of little porcelain figures, and the rather bold and modern paintings on the wall.

"What was his profession?" she asked. "How did he make a living?"

"Well, that's the interesting part about him," continued the landlady. "He was an art dealer. When we first accepted him as a tenant, I said to my husband, Egon, I said, an art dealer must be an educated and civilized person. Didn't I, Egon?" Nobody at this point expected any sort of reply from the husband, but he smiled knowingly behind half-closed eyes.

"You see, our daughter is an artist, and that's why we know many of her friends, who are artists too, and we like them all."

"Did he have a gallery?" Vega asked.

"I asked him once, thinking that he might be interested in exhibiting one of my daughter's friends. He answered rather grumpily that he conducted all his business from his office downtown."

"What kind of art did he deal in?" Vega asked, thinking of the German expressionists and French impressionists in the Max Silberberg collection.

"He said nineteenth and early twentieth century art, expressionists and such, nothing contemporary, which means no living artists."

"What kind of car did he drive?" asked Mallarmé, who had been taking notes during the entire conversation.

"He drove a blue BMW 6 series, with a V8 engine and six-speed automatic from 2002," Egon said clear as a bell. Everybody perked up in surprise, even Egon's wife.

"Thank you," Bonacourt said. "That is very helpful Herr Schmidt. How did Herr Prattler pay his rent? Do you have any financial records with his bank contacts anymore?"

Egon's wife took over again, after a tiny pause in which she seemed to recover from the shock that Egon had actually contributed to the conversation.

"Prattler paid by check each month, punctually. Actually, now that I think of it, I remember it was a Swiss bank account. I was surprised at the time, but there were never any problems, so I got used to it. Did he do anything? I mean, why do you want to know all those things?" In their friendliness and eagerness to help, it only seemed to occur to them now that the presence of the police at seven-thirty at night may have other than social reasons.

Bonacourt and Mallarmé looked at each other.

"It seems like he may have committed two murders," Bonacourt finally said.

"Egon, my God, did you hear that? I can't believe it! I always thought there was something wrong with him, but murder? I never would have imagined, not in my wildest dreams…"

"Frau Schmidt, you have been very helpful, and we apologize to giving you such a shock, but we have reason to believe that Herr Prattler is a very dangerous man. Since he moved out, did you change the locks?" Bonacourt asked calmly.

"My goodness, Egon, what should we do? No, we never thought to change the locks. We are very security conscious - we always lock the doors and windows twice at night, and when we leave the house, we even lock the windows, as a security expert from the police recommended - but we never thought it necessary to change the locks! I am so upset, I can't even think straight!"

Frau Schmidt was clearly distraught and dismayed that her kind and trusting nature could have been so misused and that they had been living in such immediate proximity to a dangerous criminal. Vega offered to get her a glass of water, which she accepted, and her husband Egon took over in a precise and deliberate manner to answer the inspector's questions.

"Herr Prattler never possessed the key to our apartment," he explained slowly, "and we have deadbolts and a chain, so I don't think we are in any immediate danger." He then reasoned logically, "In addition, Herr Prattler has left five years ago, and if he indeed made copies of our house key, as you seem to be suggesting, he could have entered this house at any point during the past years, which he hasn't. Therefore, I think the likelihood of him coming back here now, is relatively small." Frau Schmidt visibly calmed down as she listened to the slow and methodical voice of her husband.

"True," Bonacourt frowned, "but recent events have caused Prattler to take some very drastic actions. I don't think he knows of our visit here, and I certainly hope he is not aware how close we are to finding him, but I strongly suggest you use your deadbolts and chain tonight and get the locks replaced first thing in the morning. I will also call your local police station and ask them to drive by your house periodically tonight, just to be on the safe side." Herr and Frau Schmidt nodded wide-eyed. "Now, we don't want to take anymore of your time, but if it is not too much trouble we would like to take a look around Herr Prattler's apartment. You said it was empty, didn't you?

And if you could still find any of those bank records, it would be very helpful to us."

Frau Schmidt got up, her agitation now seemingly replaced by determination, and offered to show Vega and the policemen the apartment while Herr Schmidt looked for the records. They walked down the stairs to the first floor to the ongoing narrative of Frau Schmidt. Prattler's former apartment was furnished simply and had been empty most of the time during the past five years. Large, colorful and expressionistic paintings hung on every available wall.

"My daughter's art," Frau Schmidt pointed out proudly. Vega looked around in the small, well equipped, but unused kitchen.

"Inspector, look at this!" She held up a book of matches, which had been stuck between a container with tea and a strainer. The matches bore the logo of a New York City restaurant.

"Remember Sarah's letters from New York?" she asked triumphantly.

Bonacourt rolled his eyes, and Vega remembered that she was not supposed to know about the letters or their content, but at this point it did not seem to matter anymore.

"Have you or your children been to New York City lately?" Bonacourt asked Frau Schmidt.

"Not for many years. My daughter lived there for a few years; it is an important city for contemporary artists. Herr Prattler flew to New York for business quite frequently," she volunteered.

Bonacourt and Vega nodded at each other. It fit.

"Could we have these matches, Frau Schmidt" Bonacourt asked as he carefully picked up the matchbook at one corner and dropped it into an evidence bag.

"Yes, of course you can have them, but I don't think they work anymore. They have been laying here for so long. I can give you fresh matches," Frau Schmidt offered helpfully.

Bonacourt smiled. "Thank you that won't be necessary," he said. "You have been so kind and helpful. We won't bother you anymore. Just don't forget to lock your doors tonight!"

Herr Schmidt joined them and triumphantly handed a bank record to Bonacourt with the date, amount, and bank contact Prattler had paid with during his stay at Paradies Strasse.

As they made their way out into the quiet street, the old couple waved good-bye and then Bonacourt and his team heard the deadbolts turning three times in the entrance door behind them.

The roads were deserted at this time of the night, and Mallarmé pushed the Renault on the Autobahn heading back to Strasbourg to its limits, as they drove in silence, each of them following their own thoughts in the darkness.

Tuesday, May 26, Klingenthal, 8:30 AM:

One truly terrible way to start a new day is to be awakend by the persistent ringing of the telephone. As Vega tried to rise to the surface of consciousness, the ringing mingled with scraps and fragments of her dreams, turning them ugly and terrifying. Half-conscious memories of night calls announcing disaster or accidents penetrated the membrane of sleep. She groped around in the dark for her cell phone, which she had discarded the previous night before crawling into bed in the darkness, not wanting to wake her husband. Bonacourt and Mallarmé had dropped her off in front of her dark house after midnight and she had stumbled into bed exhausted. When she finally opened her eyes - tearing herself away from dream images of a kindly, gray-bearded Max Silberberg being pushed into a boxcar on his way to the concentration camp - she realized it was not early. The alarm clock showed it was eight thirty and the bed next to her was empty. Apparently her considerate husband had taken the kids to school and let her sleep.

"Hello," she groggily answered the phone.

"Good morning, Madame Stern," Mallarmé said apologetically, "I am sorry to wake you, but Bonacourt said you'd want to know."

"I wasn't sleeping," Vega lied, realizing that Mallarmé was obviously already at work and he had gotten home much later than her. "What did Bonacourt want me to know?"

"It's Jean Bonnard, the tobacco store owner," Mallarmé explained. "He is in the hospital."

Vega was suddenly wide awake.

"What happened to him? Is it serious?"

"His shop got vandalized and he was attacked viciously, while we were in Germany yesterday." Vega's heart skipped a beat. "He will be okay, eventually," continued Mallarmé, "but he does have several broken ribs, a broken jaw, a skull fracture, and a concussion."

"My God, who did this to him?" asked Vega, now sitting up straight in bed.

"A hate crime, apparently. The perpetrator left behind a racist message with spray paint on the parts of the store window he hadn't smashed: '*Socialists, Decadents and Jews will be silenced*'. He also sprayed a swastika and another symbol over the bookshelves and pictures in Bonnard's store."

"How horrible! I did not even know Bonnard was Jewish. Where is he now?"

"He is at the Hopital Civil on the Quai Louis Pasteur."

"I'll visit him and also drive by the shop and look at the symbol."

"Merci, madame," Mallarmé said brusquely, eager to go.

"And Mallarmé - thanks for letting me know." She hung up and got up cursing. Once again the early morning call had confirmed its bad reputation and brought disastrous news.

After a quick cup of coffee, Vega started the Citroen and drove straight to the Place du Temple Neuf, where she found more familiar yellow crime scene tape, this time blocking off the tobacco store. Bonacourt was there with his forensic team, and when he saw Vega's yellow car he waved her into an absolutely forbidden parking slot. Vega proudly climbed out of her car in full view of at least six uniformed police officers and joined Bonacourt in the wrecked remains of Jean Bonnard's demolished tobacco store. Packs of cigarettes and pouches of tobacco had been tipped from the shelves and scattered around the store like building blocks in a disorderly child's room after a play date. Some packages were punctured and tobacco crumbs lay like brown snow on every horizontal surface. Jean's stool had only three legs remaining, and most of the books had been ripped and spray-painted so that white pages were dispersed like drop cloth, around the store.

"It's him," Vega said to Bonacourt, pointing to the symbol of a stylized Polynesian mask, sprayed next to the swastika. "The Nazis used this symbol to advertise their degenerate art exhibition. He can't help himself, he has to show off his knowledge and art expertise, assuming that we'll never figure out who he is."

"He's bold," Bonacourt said.

"He's close," Vega responded, inspecting the damage.

"This was just a warning," Bonacourt remarked. "Our phantom was reasonably sure that Bonnard had not seen him close-up, but he wanted to make his point."

Vega summed it up. "He picked the perfect victim—intellectual, Jewish, and Socialist. But the hate crime motive is just a front."

"He knows our moves," Bonacourt considered. "He did this while we were in Germany."

"Yes, but he doesn't know we have the photo!" Vega realized suddenly. "He wouldn't have to go to all this trouble to silence and threaten a potential witness who only saw him from afar, if he knew we had the picture of him and knew his identity."

"You are right," Bonacourt admitted. "There is a warrant out for him. We were able to access his records, and we could confirm that he served in the SS and was stationed in Breslau in 1945. There, he must have confiscated the Silberberg paintings and taken a few for his own collection. He drives a blue BMW, 6 series, last registered to the Paradies Strasse address. We have a more current photo of him from the passport office. We are hesitant to make it public, for fear of the art collection. If he knows we are after him he may destroy priceless works of art."

Vega listened impassively. Suddenly it hit her with full force.

"Karl Parker and his family!" she exclaimed. "If Prattler does not know that we have the photo, he'll assume that it is still with Karl Parker in Sarah's belongings. He'll do anything in his power to retrieve it, as he has done for the past few decades, trying to take it from Sarah. Inspector, I think Karl and his family are in great danger!"

Bonacourt understood the logic immediately and got on his cell phone without hesitation. Vega watched his determined face, listened to his forceful words as he barked orders into the phone, and hoped that the people on the other end of the line were able to act fast and efficiently. She thought about Karl's little daughter Rachel, whom Sarah had loved so much, and whom she had wanted to protect from a similar fate to her own.

"I am going to Tübingen. Are you coming?" Bonacourt called to her.

"No, I think I'll leave this one up to the professionals. I have a hospital visit to pay."

Bonacourt did not hear her; he was still yelling into his cell phone.

Tuesday, May 26, Strasbourg, 11:30 AM:

As Vega entered the Hospital Civil on the *Quai Louis Pasteur* she pushed the thought of Rachel out of her mind. For once she was going to let the police take care of protecting the rest of the Parker family, and concentrate instead on one victim of Herr Prattler, who was still able to receive some comfort. She found Jean Bonnard on the second floor of the hospital, where he lay in a bed wedged between a young man, whose bleached blond hair stuck out between the white bandages encircling his head, and an elderly gentleman with his left leg in traction and encased in a white cast. Bonnard did not look much better, but instead of his arms or legs being covered, his chest and head were barely visible behind the bandages and only the upper part of his very white face looked out at the ceiling completely immobilized. Vega had to lean over him in order to enter his field of vision. She smiled at him and held up the small stack of books she had brought.

"How come I constantly have to replenish your inventory of books, even though I never ever borrow any?" she said jokingly.

"You are now appointed honorary book borrower. You can come anytime and I will lend you as many as you like for an unlimited time period," Bonnard said with effort. "Let me see the titles."

"Nietzsche, Dostoyevsky, Hesse, Mann, Kafka ... just the basics." Vega rattled off the names of the authors.

"I'll need those. It looks like I'll have plenty of time to read these again. They are good old friends, especially in times of crisis." He pointed toward the stack of books with his uninjured hand. Vega put them down in an easily reachable distance and sat down at the edge of the bed.

"What happened? Can you talk? Do you want to talk about it?" she asked.

"Yes to both," Bonnard answered quietly and began. "At about one thirty last night I was in my apartment, reading, when I heard noises in the store below. I went downstairs to investigate and when I turned on the light in the store I saw a man - black high leather boots, black face mask, black leather jacket - demolishing everything in sight. The window was already broken; that's how he got in. When I found him, he was destroying the books, the shelves, the furniture; he was like a destruction machine. He was in a rage, but he also was very methodical about it, making sure that everything he touched would be irretrievably destroyed." Bonnard paused. He spoke barely above a whisper, because he could not move his broken jaw very well.

"Take your time," said Vega. "You don't have to continue if it is too much for you."

"I want to speak about it," Jean said with effort and continued. "I shouted at him 'What are you doing? Stop!' He turned around and when he saw me he snarled and then he started to attack me, without saying a single word. He just lifted the club he carried and let it come down on me with as much force as he could. I was completely taken by surprise. He gave me no warning; there was no hesitation and no emotion. It felt like he just did what he had come to do, and that included beating me to a pulp. I don't even know if he knew who I was."

"He knew," Vega said. "He left a few clues behind. He even knew that you are Jewish."

"It is not something I advertise. Even today, being Jewish does not win you the popularity award. I remember lying on the floor, and he just kept kicking me with these black boots in the stomach and in the head. The boots were all I could see. I would recognize those boots anytime. He just kept kicking me like a robot, like I was a sack or a piece of furniture. Finally I had too much blood in my eyes to see anymore and I blacked out. I don't know what happened after that."

"Neighbors started to wake up, lights went on, people shouted on the streets and called the police. They report that the man just turned around and sprayed a mask-like symbol on the wall of your shop and then he left through the shop window, just as he came in, and drove off into the night."

"In a blue BMW?"

"Yes, and we have the registration, and the name of the driver. Jean, this was a horrible experience for you. But you will be okay. It will take a while, and it won't be easy, but you will be fine. You can get over experiences like this physically and psychologically. Plus the police are really close to catching him," Vega said comfortingly.

"I know I will be fine," Bonnard said, "and the strange thing is that I feel somehow relieved."

"It is a great relief that even though you got banged up pretty badly you are alive and you will recover!" Vega said emphatically.

"Yes, of course. But that's not what I meant. I somehow feel relieved that this happened to me. In some strange way it has restored symmetry in my life. Twenty-five years ago, I accidentally took the life of an innocent girl and I have had to live with that guilt ever since. Yesterday, a man almost killed me. For a while there, lying on the ground, I thought this is it, this is where it ends. I did nothing to that man, and what he did to me somehow seems to balance out what I did so long ago. All I tried to do was help a friend and help the police find her murderer."

"And you have. I think this is the final straw. They'll get him now. It seems that Sarah's death has transformed more than one life." Vega looked across Jean's bed out of the window at a small white cloud floating across the bright blue sky.

"Yeah, I think it's a good time for a new beginning. I don't have to sell tobacco anymore. My store is destroyed anyway. I'll do what I have always wanted and open a bookstore with a small gallery space for artists' prints."

"I'll be your first customer," Vega said as she got up to leave.

Tuesday, May 26, Tübingen: 11:55 AM:

Leah looked up at the windows of the old Tudor house in Tübingen's old town in the hope to see her daughter's blond head looking out at her. The kindergarten was almost over, and any minute now the bells would ring and the doors would open and all the children would come rushing out into the arms of their waiting parents. Mostly mothers stood on the sidewalk of Reuchlinstrasse, wicker shopping baskets on their arms, some of them with bicycles equipped with children's seats. Leah enjoyed coming here to pick up Rachel. She chatted a bit with the other mothers and found out who had chickenpox, who had a birthday party coming up, and who had found the best piano teacher. But most of all she looked forward to walking home with her daughter and talking about Rachel's day and whatever else was on her daughter's mind. One lonely father, probably a teacher or graduate student, stood off to the side, wearing sandals and jeans, waiting, but not interacting with the mothers. Leah thought about Karl, who had picked up his daughter maybe once or twice, when Leah had been sick with the flue. Karl, who flew off to New York on a wild goose chase, despite her protests, and then got mugged there. Karl, whose dead sister Sarah seemed more important to him than his living family. He loved his daughter, she was sure of it, but he could only deal with her in small doses: He took her to the playground, or gave her a bath, but in the evenings he did not want to be disturbed when he sat in his office and worked. Meanwhile Rachel and Leah were in the kitchen preparing dinner or working on projects. Leah enjoyed baking cookies and drawing pictures, but she had a master's degree in philosophy as well, and sometimes she felt like her brain was drying up and shrinking. The clock in the market place struck twelve o'clock and the bells of the cathedral began to toll. The arched wooden gates of the building burst open and the children spilled into the little front yard, where the mothers scooped them up in their arms. Rachel came skipping over to her mother, wearing a bell-shaped red skirt, which made her look a bit like little red riding hood.

"Let's walk by the river and the *Hölderlin Turm*, Mom, and feed the ducks!" she said eagerly as she slipped her hand into her mother's.

"Okay, but what about lunch?"

"That's what I mean: the ducks have to eat lunch."

"Alright, but first tell me what did you learn today?"

"I don't remember, but I found a new friend."

"That's great. Who is it and what's her name?"

"Her name is June. Isn't that a pretty name?'

"Yes, is she a new kid in your class?"

"She is not a kid, Mom."

"Oh no? What is she?"

"She is a June bug, of course. Get it? June, June bug?"

"Yes, I get it. So she is your new friend?"

"Yes, I trained her. She can do tricks and everything. I am a very good June bug trainer."

"I believe that. What kind of tricks?"

"She can hold on to my fingers with two legs only and she can make summersaults. It's amazing!"

"That is amazing! You are not hurting her or anything?"

"No, of course not. She can just fly away if she does not like it. But I am sure she'll come back tomorrow, because she likes me so much."

"Yes, I would hope so."

"She's never had such a good teacher before."

They reached the curb of the Nauklerstrasse, a fairly busy street and had to pause for the traffic. Rachel looked left and right, and a stream of cars came from both sides.

Leah thought about the ultimatum she had presented to Karl. She wanted him to be more attentive to her and Rachel. She wanted more support, so she could go and finish her Ph.D. She wanted him to let go of his obsession with Sarah. Now that Sarah was dead it had gotten worse, rather than better. Karl seemed to think he was some kind of Sherlock Holmes or something, as if the police needed him to catch the murderer, as if they had waited for a philosophy professor to solve their crime. It was ridiculous. He seemed to think that the capture was now imminent. She did not want to hear about it anymore. For years she had had to listen to his stories about Sarah. How she needed him and how he could not let her down, even though he was the younger brother. As if she and Rachel did not need him as well. She was tired of nagging, and that's why she had given him the ultimatum. He could not possibly choose the dead woman over her, or could he? Sometimes he acted so cold to her that she was not sure about his feelings for her anymore. She was not sure about her own feelings for him.

There finally was a gap in the traffic flow and they crossed, Rachel skipping and jumping next to her. They walked on the sidewalk of a quieter, residential street. It was a one-way street like so many of the narrow medieval lanes in Tübingen. Rachel skipped along with one foot on and the other off the left sidewalk. The houses were gray and so was the sky. But in the narrow spaces between the buildings lilac bushes bloomed, their violet flower bushels strangely florescent in these gray surroundings. Leah's cell phone rang. She dug in her big shoulder bag for it, while her heart made a little jump. This would be Karl, she thought. He would give her his answer now. This call could determine the direction of her life from here on. She had no idea how right this assessment was.

"Rachel, darling, run along, I'll catch up with you. I just have to talk to daddy on the phone for a minute!" she called to her daughter, Rachel turned around briefly and skipped on.

"Leah Parker here!"

"Frau Parker, this is Commisario Generell Bonacourt from the Strasbourg police."

"Why are you calling me? What is the matter? How did you get this phone number? Did something happen to Karl?"

"Frau Parker, please remain calm, nothing happened to your husband. I am calling as a precaution. We are sending a local police guard to your apartment for your protection. Please remain in the apartment until he arrives."

"Why, what is the matter? Why do we need protection?" Leah called into the receiver.

"Are you at home right now?" asked Bonacourt with a calm voice in broken German.

"No, I am walking home with my daughter. I just picked her up from Kindergarten."

"Just keep your daughter in your sight at all times; when you reach home an officer should be waiting for you there. Don't be alarmed; this is just for your protection."

"Protection from what? What are you talking about?" Leah's mind raced. Was the whole world going crazy? Were they all seeing phantoms now?

"A blue BMW, we have the license plate number. It belongs to a criminal whom we have reason to believe might try to pay you a visit,"

Bonacourt said, getting frustrated, because he obviously could not get his point across.

"A blue BMW?" Leah looked up. A blue BMW had just pulled up beside her daughter about thirty meters ahead of her on the sidewalk. The driver's door opened, and as Leah looked in frozen horror, a pair of arms reached out and grabbed her daughter and pulled her into the car.

"Rachel! My daughter! Stop him! He's kidnapping my daughter!" she screamed and ran toward the car, only to see it speeding away with screeching tires. The cell phone dropped to the ground.

"Frau Parker? Frau Parker?" Bonacourt yelled, "What happened?" All he heard was a crunch and static noise as the phone bumped and shattered on the sidewalk.

Tuesday, May 26, Strasbourg: 12:10 PM:

Bonacourt stared at the useless cell phone in his hand and cursed. The few times the damned things actually really could make a difference they were either broken or turned off. Well, at least his phone was still functioning. He quickly called an emergency number of the Tübingen police station. Mallarmé had already alerted them, and when they heard the word *kidnapping* together with the description and license plate number of the car, they were on their way. Bonacourt hung up and stood there suddenly feeling very useless. What was he going to do? If he started driving toward the border now, it would take him hours to get across and crawl on the Autobahn through thick traffic. He looked around at the devastated tobacco shop behind him, kicking some shards of broken glass aside. He looked around him at the yellow crime scene tape that seemed to entangle him and trap him like a spider web. Now a little girl was in grave danger. A little girl that the dead woman had tried so hard to protect. Sarah had wanted to prevent the vicious cycle from repeating itself, the cycle that had held her captive for the better part of her life. Sarah Parker had been an abused child and she had run away from the reality of its consequences by moving from city to city and by trying to dull her pain with drugs. Bonacourt had to do everything in his power to prevent that another young life would be wasted that way. He looked up into the gray, over cast

219

sky. Of course, he thought, why hadn't it occurred to him before!! He took a big breath and began to run. It would take too long to reach the Strasbourg Central Police Headquarters by car. On second thought, however, he considered as he jogged along breathlessly, this run might cost him a heart attack. He felt every helping of Mme. Merrier's onion tart and rhubarb cake and decided for the fifth time this year to start exercising and to get back into shape. "Lives depend on it," he muttered to himself, drawing suspicious and concerned glances from the passers by, "mine and that of Rachel Parker." When he finally burst into the police station, red-faced and breathing very heavily, the young constable on duty looked up from his newspaper with a bemused and indulgent expression.

"Monsieur, what can we do for you?" he asked with exquisite politeness.

"Bonacourt, commisario generell, Hagenau," Bonacourt huffed and stumbled toward the constable, while he searched for the identification papers in his pocket.

The constable looked at the pitiful old man in front of him with ice blue and completely indifferent eyes.

"I need a helicopter," Bonacourt declared.

"Mais oui, Monsieur," the young man responded pleasantly, "we all need many things. I for one really need a new car—" Bonacourt interrupted him by hitting his fist onto the counter.

"This," he barked, "is a matter of life and death, not a time for feeble jokes!" he bellowed. The young officer looked at him with real concern. If this madman had appeared like a good candidate for a heart attack when he stumbled into the station, his chances to come to an untimely end seemed to have tripled with this latest outburst.

"Of course," he said obligingly, "a matter of life and death."

"Where are your helicopters?" Bonacourt had caught his breath and was steel-faced now.

"Monsieur, we only have one helicopter here and that one is mainly reserved for the European Parliament, to fly government representatives to the assemblies—"

"Spare me the details! The life of a little girl is at stake!"

"Commisario," the constable began again, glancing at the identification papers, "the use of a helicopter has to be properly authorized. I can show you the forms. A registered pilot has to be secured—"

"Who authorizes it?" bellowed Bonacourt.

"At the moment that would be detective Garand, but he is in a meeting."

"Garand! Get him, now! Or you'll regret it for the rest of your career!" Bonacourt snapped.

"If you insist!" the young constable turned around and left in search of detective Garand, head held high, in an attempt to maintain some dignity, and glad to get away from this crazy maniac. Meanwhile, Bonacourt tried to collect his thoughts and devise a strategy. He knew this confrontation was not going to be easy and he did not have much time. Already Garand marched in, bristling with indignation.

"Bonacourt! You again! I should have known! How dare you come in here and make demands! I was interrupted in a very important meeting…"

"And I am interrupting you again," Bonacourt interrupted. "We know where the killer is, we have the license plate numbers of his car, and he has a hostage."

"Now all we need is a helicopter. It's that easy, is it? Inspector Bonacourt will just fly in with his magic helicopter and sweep the hostage away, leaving the potential murderer behind, bound and gagged for the foot soldiers of the police force to collect. I am surprised you are not wearing your Batman cape!" concluded Garand with a contemptuous glance at Bonacourt's battered appearance.

"Garand, your cheap cynicism may cost a four year old girl her life!" said Bonacourt sadly.

"All due to your incredible incompetence. Your entire investigation is a disgrace to the entire police force. How do you suddenly claim to know about the location of the killer?"

"Because I talked to the mother in Tübingen, when the girl was kidnapped. Please Garand, I beg you, I plead with you, if I have to. We should not let personal rivalries get in the way of rescuing an innocent child. We have already lost precious minutes arguing. As we speak the killer is escaping, driving out of our range!"

"And how do you know the kidnapper is actually identical to the killer of Madame Gluck?" Bonacourt sighed.

"Because Madame Gluck was about to give his description to the police. He is the man in the blue BMW, and as Vega Stern pointed out, he is after the evidence, which he suspects to be in Karl Parker's possession."

"Ah, Vega Stern, I read her name in your reports. What does she have to do with all this? An amateur, an art historian! How can you allow someone like that to be involved in the investigation? Do you realize what that means? If it should come to a trial, any evidence collected by or connected to this woman would be thrown out of court! Such unprofessional sloppy procedures will cost you your head sooner or later!" he finished with satisfaction.

"Okay, Garand," intercepted Bonacourt, who had been checking his watch during Garand's outburst, "I offer you a deal: You can have my head on a silver platter. If anything goes wrong, and if we don't catch Prattler, I'll hand you my badge personally. Just give me that helicopter, now!" Garand hesitated, obviously picturing Bonacourt's head being presented to him à la Salome and John the Baptist.

"If there is as much as a scratch on the helicopter?" he persisted.

"I'll take care of the scratch," Bonacourt promised

"It will take you almost an hour to fly to Tübingen!"

"Then I better get going now!"

"Not you, WE are going. I am coming with you, Bonacourt, I am watching you!" triumphed Garand as they filed out the back of the station, under the incredulous eyes of the young constable.

Tuesday, May 26, Strasbourg: 12:45 PM:

As Vega stepped out of the hospital doors, she felt optimistic about Jean Bonnard's recovery. He'd be alright. Maybe even better than before. Vega did not want to credit Prattler with the change in Bonnard, but instead she attributed it to the transforming powers of Sarah. As she looked up into the gray sky above the Quai St. Nicolas she suddenly felt a chill running down her spine. She shuddered and looked around for an explanation of this unexpected coldness that felt like it could freeze her blood. What had happened? Her first thought went to her children. Were they safe? She rushed to her car and drove to the international school even though it was much too early to pick them up. She parked the car on the street and just sat there, watching the entrance and a glimpse of Daniel's classroom window. Everything looked calm and normal. But Vega still felt uneasy. How could her mood change so quickly and so completely from one minute to the other? She decided to call her husband on her cell phone.

"Vega, good timing!" her husband Greg said, "Mallarmé just called. Prattler apparently kidnapped the little girl, Rachel!" A wave of despair broke over Vega.

"Oh my god," she stammered. "We were too late. He was one step ahead of us."

"Don't worry, Mallarmé said, they have the license plate number and the description and the police is on full alert in Tübingen. He won't get far!"

But of course Vega did worry, and she did not let the school entrance gate out of her sight until she saw her sons emerge from it.

Tuesday, May 26, Tübingen: 1 PM:

Karl Parker closed the Nietzsche text *Human, All Too Human*, which he had discussed with his class and dismissed the students. They had been restless, and wondered if he had been unable to convey the meaning of Nietzsche's writing sufficiently or if it was the gray day and the anticipation for lunch that had caused the students to shuffle their feet and slide around on their seats. He sighed. In part three of *Human All Too Human* Nietzsche quotes Lord Byron in agreement:

"Sorrow is knowledge: They who know the most must mourn the deepest o'er the fatal truth, the Tree of Knowledge is not that of Life."

Teaching and studying philosophy had never made anybody happy. The more one understands of life, the more painful it becomes. Karl tried not to think of his sister Sarah and her particular torment; instead he tore himself out of his reverie and stuffed his papers into the briefcase. He would have to go home and face Leah and her ultimatum. He had avoided thinking of it. Of course he chose his living family over his dead sister, but he did not like the strings Leah had attached to his decision. He felt for the first time in years that he was actually contributing to solving Sarah's murder and her mystery. He felt, if he could just see this case through, it would give him great freedom and relief. Why couldn't Leah see that? Why was she so jealous of his sister, now as badly or worse than when she was still alive? He did not want his daughter to grow up without any memories of her aunt. Rachel and Sarah had adored each other. He did not want to agree to a strict no-mentioning-of-Sarah's-name-policy in his own house, as Leah had demanded. She wanted to go back to University to get her doctorate. Fine, but couldn't she just wait until Rachel was in school? He shook his head and stepped out of the classroom, where a uniformed policeman immediately intercepted him. His students stood close by watching and trying to overhear the reason for this unusual visit of law enforcement at the philosophy department.

"What is this all about?" Karl Parker demanded, "Can we step outside?"

Taking the police officer's arm and leading him out the door and down the steps of the Alte Burse Building, out of his students' earshot.

"Herr Parker, I am very sorry," the officer began, and he indeed felt very sorry, "but your daughter has been kidnapped." He winced as he saw the blood drain out of Parker's face. "For your own protection and in order to enable you to be a part of the pursuit of the perpetrator, we suggest you remain in my presence," he soldiered on. Parker still seemed paralyzed and frozen on the spot on the third step of the building. So the officer continued:

"The entire old town is sealed off with road blocks, a regional alert went out with the license plate number and the car description, he won't get far!" almost pleading now.

"Yes, of course. Where is my wife?" whispered Karl. Suddenly Leah's image emerged hugely in his mind. If he was in shock and suffering right now, she would feel a hundred times worse.

"Your wife is at police headquarters. She was walking you daughter home from Kindergarten when it happened—"

"He took her in the middle of the day, in the middle of the street, in the middle of town?" Parker asked incredulous.

227

"Yes, Sir, I am sorry to say, but as I mentioned—"

"Prattler, of course. He thinks I have the picture. He is using Rachel to get it back."

"That's what we assume, Sir."

"But I don't even have it! The whole thing is senseless, it is completely unnecessary, it is inhuman, it is irrational, he does not even know, that I don't have it?"

"We know, Herr Parker, but we have his identity. It won't be long. If you don't mind coming with me, you'll be right there when we stop him and free your daughter."

Karl Parker allowed himself to be led away, suddenly stooped over like a man three times his age.

Tuesday, May 26, Tübingen, 1:30 PM:

From up in the air Bonacourt's eyes followed the silver-gray band of the Neckar until it wound its way into the old town center of Tübingen, underneath Neckar bridge, passing Hölderlinturm on the right and then flowing lazily past the castle hill, with Hohentübingen from the seventeenth century on top. The tower was much older than the rest of the castle. It looked proud and sturdy and undefeatable from this vantage point. The noise of the helicopter was deafening, but Bonacourt did not mind. It had gotten him where he needed to be in less than an hour, and now he had the grand view of the little university town, where all eyes stared at them, because helicopters were not a common sight over these medieval streets. Bonacourt scanned the roads, and noticed a roadblock near the train station, at one of the roads leading out of town. Good, he thought. Hopefully Prattler hadn't slipped out yet. If he were still inside the city, he would run into their net, unless his home was right in town, which Bonacourt doubted. It would have taken Prattler some time to bind the girl, speculated Bonacourt, hoping that the man had not resorted to more brutal measures. As the helicopter circled the castle hill showing the dramatic Hohentübingen Castle with its ornate entrance gate, from its most attractive angle, Bonacourt suddenly felt like he was playing a part in a movie. He had the surreal feeling of participating in the picturesque introduction to the unavoidable car chase scene. The movie approached its climax as the united police forces hunted down the criminal from the air and from the ground in a dramatic finale. But this was no movie, as detective Garand, who sat next to him and yelled over the noise of the helicopter, rudely reminded him:

"Where is your criminal now?" This was reality and the little girl Rachel had to be foremost on his mind; therefore he ignored the rude question and answered calmly:

"We will see him soon, I am sure." This was no time for bravado, but instead he had to proceed with utter caution, if he wanted to avoid endangering the young hostage's life. Prattler was unpredictable, and Bonacourt did not want him to loose his head or his temper. As far as Bonacourt knew, he did not have a gun; all his crimes had been committed with a knife. A sharp knife, which he obviously yielded skillfully; a knife that he did not want to come in any contact with little Rachel. Bonacourt took a deep breath to calm down his breathing and to concentrate fully on the observation of the narrow roads below, winding through the dark pines and lime green beech trees of the Schönbuch Forest. Garand next to him was growing impatient. Suddenly he spotted a blue car moving in a Northwestern direction away from Tübingen toward the Black Forest. He adjusted his binoculars, pointed it out to Garand and told the pilot to move in closer to confirm the identity of the blue BMW. Through his headphones and mike, he established contact with officer Haupt on the ground. To facilitate communication, they spoke English.

"Bonacourt here. I am fairly sure I spotted the fugitive. He is on the B28 moving toward Herrenberg. He is already past the roadblocks. Pursue immediately but with caution. Do not do anything that could provoke the suspect. We must avoid any danger to the hostage. Over."

A bit distorted by static, but clearly audible, Haupt responded from the ground:

"Copy. I have the parents with me. Please update us on the location of the fugitive's car. I will alert the police forces in the surrounding villages and in Herrenberg. Over." He had to be careful what to say, thought Bonacourt. He appreciated Haupt's warning about Rachel's parents being with him. He did not want to say anything they could interpret in the wrong way and that would send them into an emotional tailspin. At that moment he saw the car turn off the Bundesstasse onto a small road leading south.

"Haupt, Bonacourt here again. The car just made a turn south, toward Rottenburg, according to my map here."

"He is leading us to his house, which is probably full of stolen art work!" exclaimed Garand excitedly, suddenly caught up in the thrill of the chase. Bonacourt immediately bridled his enthusiasm, and reminded him of Rachel. They could not risk following Prattler all the way home, not if it meant leaving Rachel in his company any longer than absolutely necessary.

"Haupt here. We could intercept in Rottenburg at the first traffic light. Pretend it is a routine traffic check and then pull him and the girl out," Haupt suggested.

Leah and Karl looked at each other. They sat tensely in the backseat of the patrol car, their bodies as rigid as boards. At the mention of their daughter, Leah gasped quietly and Karl grabbed her arm, either as a gesture of comfort or to prevent her from loosing control of herself.

"Can you guarantee that the traffic light is red?" snapped Bonacourt form the air. "If it isn't, he's just going to sail right through."

"No, we cannot guarantee that," admitted Haupt. "But we can create a traffic obstacle with another car pretending to be disabled, blocking the road, emergency blinkers on, and an officer directing and stopping traffic," he suggested.

"Better," bellowed Bonacourt. "He seems to be going straight for the village. There is only one road through town. Contact your colleagues at once and set it up!" he demanded like a commander in a battle.

"We'll try our best," responded Haupt, dialing already, but he was interrupted by a sharp voice from above.

"You are not just going to try, you will bloody well succeed!"

Bonacourt's adrenaline was pumping now and he knew they had very little time and very little room for error, as long as Prattler was still rolling toward the small town, unaware that he was being observed and followed.

In the patrol car Leah flinched at the sharp tone of Bonacourt's voice, and Karl automatically put his hand over hers. He squeezed her fingers almost painfully, but she was grateful for any distraction from the tension unfolding in the chase. Haupt was already on the radio with police officers in Rottenburg and gave them instructions to set up the trap.

"So far he is not suspecting that we are on his trail, so don't do anything rash, we don't want him to panic and react violently," Haupt instructed the village officers, who had never had so much excitement in their entire careers and were not very well prepared for a hostage-car-chase-ake-over! Karl, who listened from the backseat, was aware of their inexperience, and Leah could see his face going pale, and the knuckles on his hands turned white.

"Bonacourt here. I estimate you have approximately eight minutes time before he arrives. So don't waste it. Out."

"Eight minutes!" Haupt yelled into the mike. "Go now! When he stops, close in from both sides at once, in case the girl is right next to him. Pull her out first. We do not expect him to have a gun, but he knows how to handle a knife. Good luck! You can do it!" Haupt wiped the sweat from his forehead and started the car. Leah looked out of the window at the green meadow beyond and suddenly a memory flash of her daughter flooded her mind. Rachel, in her little pink rubber boots, running across the grass toward her, showing her two little ladybugs she had caught, with utter delight, a great proud smile on her shiny face. "Rachel!" she whispered. Karl let go of her hand and instead put his arm around her shoulder, pulling her closer toward him.

"The BMW is entering the village," Bonacourt reported from the sky. "He stopped at the road block. The officers are approaching the car. There is one officer on each side. One officer talks to the driver. The other officer is trying to open the passenger door. It seems to be locked. Open the driver's door, damn it! There is a commotion. The first officer reaches in and opens the driver's door. He grabs the driver and pulls him out. Two more officers approach and restrain him. The other officer opens the passenger door. I can see him reaching in. He comes out carrying a little girl. It's Rachel, she is on her feet, she seems fine! The officer removes her gag and the rope from her hands. She is okay; she is following him to the patrol car. Prattler is struggling but under control. It's over. She's safe!" Bonacourt broke off his narrative, the excitement and relief too much to express.

"They officers have Prattler handcuffed! WE got him!" added Garand proudly.

Haupt looked around to Karl and Leah, while he started the car. At first they sat completely still, as if frozen, then as the news sank in, he saw them starting to laugh with relief and finally fall into each other's arms.

"We'll be there in five minutes!" he said, but they did not hear him.

"Rachel! Rachel!" Leah kept calling. The radio came to life again.

"Here is Rachel," a police officer's voice said. "She has a message for her parents." Then Rachel's tiny voice came through the loudspeaker:

"Hi Mom, hi Dad. Don't worry about me. I am fine. Love you both! See you soon!"

The connection broke off. Leah and Karl looked at each other, enormously relieved. How trivial and unimportant their quarrels and the silly ultimatum now seemed, how utterly immature and childish. They had needed their daughter and this horrible incident to remind them about what really mattered. Leah started to cry and then to sob and Karl held her and stroked her hair, as Haupt sped through the forest, much faster than the speed limit allowed.

Wednesday, May 27, Klingenthal, 8 AM:

The first timid rays of morning sun stretched across the room and woke Vega, who was still laying on the sofa, with Stevie's small body curled up besides her, breathing deeply. Carefully she got up and tiptoed to the door, to retrieve the *Strasbourg Daily*. Sitting at the kitchen table she found the article on page 2 under the headline:

Kidnapper, Art Thief and Suspected Killer Arrested

In an unprecedented co-operation between the French and German police, wanted kidnapper, art thief, and suspected murderer Fritz Prattler was brought to justice yesterday in a dramatic car chase through the Black Forest. The suspect was stopped and apprehended by the police between Tübingen and Herrenberg around 1:45 on Tuesday May 26. At the time of his arrest he held four-year old Rachel P. hostage and was trying to reach his home in an abandoned mill in a remote forest valley. The young hostage is unharmed, but Mr. Prattler is accused of the murder of the German woman Sarah Parker (35) who was found dead on the Mont Ste Odile earlier this month. Police suspect the murder is connected to the killing of the Strasbourg boarding house owner Gisele Gluck (67), who was found dead in her bed on Sunday this week. Mme. Gluck owned the boarding house where Ms Parker stayed. On the suspects estate police found over 40 pieces of valuable artwork, much of it looted during and before WWII from Jewish collectors. One painting was identified as a Paul Klee work, formerly belonging to the Jewish collector Max Silberberg, from Breslau. Max Silberberg had lost his considerable art collection due to Nazi confiscation and he subsequently perished in a concentration camp. The Strasbourg Daily reached his son Alfred Silberberg in London by phone. He was overjoyed about the recovery.

"We had already given up on seeing any of my father's paintings ever again. After all these years it is like a wonderful and unexpected surprise, that these works that meant so much to my father have been recovered." He said in a statement to the press.

The artwork will be returned to its rightful heir later this year. Detective Inspector Garand, head of the Strasbourg police department is very pleased with the outcome of the rescue operation:

"I had to make some difficult decisions, while Fritz Prattler was on the run with his young victim. A life and death situation like that requires fast and decisive action, and that is exactly what we did, cutting red tape, securing a helicopter, and working together with our colleagues from across the border. Today is a proud day for the entire Strasbourg police force!" Details about the trial have not been released to date.

The article was accompanied by the picture of a smashing looking middle-aged man in a well-cut three-piece suit, pointing proudly at the Paul Klee painting. The subtitle identified him as: Detective-Inspector Garand in front of one of the recovered art works.

Vega looked at the picture with a frown. The Klee was the same as the backdrop in the photo of Prattler and his brother, this time partially obstructed by the expansive gesture of Garand. She was incredibly relieved that Rachel had apparently come out of the ordeal without a scratch, and that the art was recovered, but who in the world was this Garand? She had never heard of him and why was there no mention of Bonacourt? It did not make any sense. Stevie woke up and tugged on her arm.

"Mom, don't we have to go to school soon?"

"Yes, of course, sorry. I just read in the paper that the police caught the killer of the dead girl on the mountain."

"Did you help them catch him, Mom?"

"I hope so."

"I'll tell her ghost. She'll be so relieved, and she won't have to haunt our house anymore."

"Has she been doing that, lately?"

"Not too bad, I got used to it. But I think we really should go to school now."

"I agree, Stevie. Let's get going."

Monday, June 1, Klingenthal, 4 PM:

Vega sat in her office in front of the computer. Finally she was writing and it did not feel like torture. Stevie looked over her shoulder on to the screen and read:

> *Despite the fog it was going to be a wonderful day. Vega was determined to make it so, as she trudged down the sodden forest path, wet leaves squishing under her soles. She was living her dream, in the country of her dreams, pursuing a story she had chosen to write about the ancient abbess Ste Odile, who used to reside on this mountain in the Alsace in France. On clear days Vega could see the Rhine Valley, the Black Forest in Germany, and the spire of the Strasbourg Cathedral in France from here. Today she could barely see the next oak tree along the slippery path before bumping into it. She arrived at the Spring of Tears, where healing waters sprang from the rocks and left them glistening and wet. Vega watched the stream of water bursting from the rock and then disappear again between stones and leaves. Suddenly something pink and pointy between the twigs and wet leaves caught her eye. The bright pink object stood out like a neon sign amidst colors in variations of green, brown, rust and gray earth tones. Vega stepped closer. The object*

was triangular and sharp edged, and the closer she came, the clearer she could see that it had very elegant lines indeed.

ABOUT THE AUTHOR:

Cornelia Feye received her M.A. in Art History and Anthropology from the University of Tübingen, Germany. She taught Eastern and Western Art History at several colleges including Mesa College, Grossmont College, Miracosta College and UCSD in San Diego. Her museum experience includes curating a Tibet Exhibition at the Mingei International Museum and being a museum educator at the Jacques Marchais Museum of Tibetan Art in New York, as well as the San Diego Museum of Man and the California Center for the Arts, Escondido. She was Manager of Docent programs at the San Diego Museum of Art for six years and is currently the School of the Arts and Arts Education Director at the Athenaeum Music & Arts Library in La Jolla. She manages over 40 art instructors who teach art classes at two campuses in La Jolla and San Diego. Her publications include art historical essays and reviews in English and German.

11812118R00131

Made in the USA
Charleston, SC
22 March 2012